I'm Not Alice,
I'm Alice

I'm Not Alice, I'm Alice

ONE FAMILY'S JOURNEY WITH AUTISM

Beverly Tucker

MARINER
PUBLISHING

BUENA VISTA, VA

1 3 5 7 9 10 8 6 4 2

Library of Congress Control Number: 2014952646
I'm Not Alice, I'm Alice
By Beverly Tucker

p. cm.
1. Fiction: Autism
2. Fiction: Family Life
3. Fiction: 20th Century Virginia

I. Tucker, Beverly, 1938— II. Title.
ISBN 13: 978-0-9849214-9-2 (softcover : alk. paper)

Edited by Judy Rogers and Karen Bowen

Cover and Book Design by Emilie Davis

Mariner Media, Inc.
131 West 21st Street
Buena Vista, VA 24416
Tel: 540-264-0021
www.marinermedia.com

Printed in the United States of America

This book is printed on acid-free paper meeting the
requirements of the American Standard for Permanence of Paper
for Printed Library Materials.

Eternal

Means no time,

no end

Do your children

who visit you in time

really reside in eternity?

If you try to grasp them,

they slip away.

They are more than what you see and hear and feel.

They belong somewhere else

and only visit you here.

So why do you worry?

—Rumi
13th century Persian mystic

Table of Contents

Preface

I'm Not Alice, I'm Alice is based on the life experiences of a real family. I have observed the difficulties, challenges, and decisions that face this family and honor their ongoing effort of attempting to understand and even celebrating the differences of an autistic child. They are daily "committed to creating a place on this earth where their child may feel comfortable."

The artwork included in the Appendix was created by the autistic child of this family. I selected from stacks of drawings those that seemed to follow the story line. What appears to be lines, circles, and scribbles convey the creation of images of people and events. There is an element of confusion on initial viewing, but then the work comes alive with movement and clarity of meaning.

The title for the book, *I'm Not Alice, I'm Alice*, represents the unpredictable, even uncanny, expression of thought often related to autism.

This book is dedicated with love and admiration, to this extraordinary family. May they all live in that special place of acceptance.

The Family Trees

THE BURKES

Aunt Mary Caitlin *(Mrs. Burke's sister)*	Mrs. Burke	Mr. Burke

THE O'MALLEYS

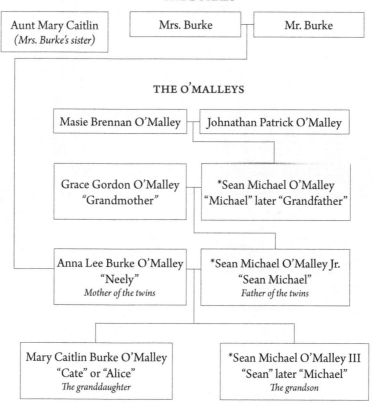

Masie Brennan O'Malley	Johnathan Patrick O'Malley

Grace Gordon O'Malley "Grandmother"	*Sean Michael O'Malley "Michael" later "Grandfather"

Anna Lee Burke O'Malley "Neely" *Mother of the twins*	*Sean Michael O'Malley Jr. "Sean Michael" *Father of the twins*

Mary Caitlin Burke O'Malley "Cate" or "Alice" *The granddaughter*	*Sean Michael O'Malley III "Sean" later "Michael" *The grandson*

* A clarification of the three generations with the same name.

THE DRUMMONDS

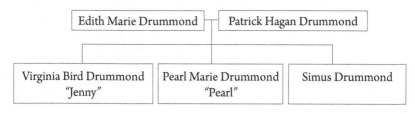

Edith Marie Drummond	Patrick Hagan Drummond

Virginia Bird Drummond "Jenny"	Pearl Marie Drummond "Pearl"	Simus Drummond

Chapter One

Gazing through the wavy four-over-four window panes, one could see that the snow had melted and the grass was again visible. It wasn't pretty grass, but rather the same grayish brown of the deer pack that wandered in each day to munch their way through what was left of the burning bushes. It was as if the grass belonged to them, and they were merely loaning it to those who lived there in the old house with the tall chimneys. The daily fires, so generously provided for by the surrounding woods, were not only for warming the rooms with their high ceilings but for the glow that embraced the papered walls and the hands that so carefully gathered the kindling. The view out the window held promise of a new season in which the fires would be gratefully exchanged for the planting and gathering of the green beans and zinnias. The *Farmers' Almanac* had issued the initial warning for a severe winter featuring a menu of snow and ice. The farmers know these things.

Cate had heard talk of the almanac's prognostication with a shiver that lasted throughout the long dark days. She may have thought of the friendly sound of the cowbells. Their music down in the meadow always seemed to announce the arrival of spring. The jingle could be easily and often heard from the screened porch at the back of the house. The porch was a favorite place for Cate to spend most of her warmer hours; she seemed to take pleasure in the screen's adamant exclusion of the summer mosquitoes. The drone of the cicadas provided a bass string section to the percussion of the cowbells' symphony. Though loud, the cicadas were also mesmerizing and often prompted Cate to nod off for maybe a minute. It was just part of a summer afternoon on the porch.

That early spring morning, Cate's thoughts might have focused on the subtle hints suggested by the tiny buds on the tulip trees or perhaps she imagined from their teasing that they would soon bloom if she were patient. This was unlikely, for she was never patient. Cate's best friend Jenny reminded her of the possibility of late April snow flurries but reassured her that they were likely over. Cate accepted Jenny's optimism. They took hope from past spring seasons' inevitable arrivals. Cate had a vague notion of the fickle nature of the weather, which was as much a reality as her life and the puzzles within it. Was she aware of those puzzles? Probably not…It was simply her life and she knew no other.

Her real name was Mary Caitlin Burke O'Malley. She was southern through and through by virtue of birth, but she had never embraced the traditional notion of her double name. In fact, she likely did not recognize tradition. It was actually Jenny who suggested shortly after Mary Caitlin was born that this little girl should be called Cate. "That long name from the auntie is just too much name for such a tiny little thing," Jenny declared. Jenny knew the story behind the choice of that name, but she had managed to convince Cate's mother that this was more practical on a daily basis. But now Cate was nine, and she could decide on a special name to be used by those people she trusted.

She had her ways of showing her approval and disapproval. For those few that she really, really trusted, she had chosen a special name of her own. That choice was "Alice." No one was sure why. Jenny had observed as Cate had sorted through possibilities in her own way, which was to lie on her stomach and write names in various configurations for her consideration. Written with colorful markers, in capital letters only, she translated her experience with possibilities. Names under consideration were:

CAITLIN BURKE OMALLEY, MARY ALICE BURKE OMALLEY, MARY IRIS BURKE OMALLEY, MARY

CAITLIN, CAITLIN BURKE, CATE BURKE, CATE ALICE, CATE IRIS, CATE IRIS ALICE, IRIS OMALLEY

After narrowing the list to just "Alice" and "Iris," she settled on "Alice." Iris had been a possibility that made sense as it was her favorite flower. It grew in abundance in the garden of one of her most trusted friends, Miss Ava Rankin, an artist who had introduced Cate to the joy of flowers. They had spent hours in that beautiful garden learning how to communicate in color. Cate favored blues and greens and reds, depending on what she intended to express. Miss Ava was most surely one of those special people to whom Cate would give permission and say in her own unique way, "Thank you, please call me Alice," or "I'm not Alice, I'm Alice."

Most people honored her wishes to be called Cate, that is everyone except her mother Neely O'Malley, who had to be convinced. This convincing, Jenny took upon herself. Neely had carefully chosen the name of Mary Caitlin because it had belonged to her favorite aunt. Aunt Mary Caitlin had since gone to her great reward, and this was Neely's way of honoring her revered auntie in the afterlife. Still, the namesake was not fond of the choice. Cate had never had the pleasure of making her great-aunt's acquaintance, but it likely wouldn't have made any difference. Still she was curious about where that dear lady had gone.

She was curious about those family members who had died and where they were now. She was curious about heaven. Neely explained that Aunt Mary Caitlin had gone to heaven, "the next planet," where our souls go after our bodies die on earth. Cate was very interested in whether or not her progenitors could now jump and fly in heaven. Neely explained that they could indeed jump and fly and do wonderful things.

Cate often asked, "Can I go to heaven?"

"Not now," Neely replied, "Not now."

Cate really liked the O'Malley part of her name but could barely remember about Burke or its origin. She had been told it had something to do with her mother's side of the family, and she may have felt they had been remembered enough.

O'Malley was rooted in the fascinating family lore of her paternal ancestors and the beauty of their place of origin. To Cate, those family stories were magical. They were an essential part of her fabric, woven with threads of the past, that were her heritage but not her reality. No one was sure of her reality.

Neely believed that Cate included those family stories in her stacks of art and, as Miss Ava had taught Cate, she could express those stories. When thinking about those images that she really loved, Cate seemed to use the greenest of greens and bluest of blues. It was red that expressed her anger and anxiety. In fact, it was color that ultimately became an essential element of her language.

The valley where she lived provided the illusion of living in the womb of those beautiful blue mountains. She seemed to respond with joy. She did not speak of it, unless it was in the sounds or deeds to which she had access. There were times when she did not access what she knew.

Her experience in the real womb of her mother had not been so pleasant, her reticence now perhaps a result of that time. If she could have spoken from that womb's safe place, she might have revealed that her early restlessness was the result of another someone sharing that precious yet crowded space.

Chapter Two

In Cate's world, words sometimes came out of order, but Jenny Drummond explained things. So it was that after their lengthy discussion of the approaching spring, they made their way to the kitchen. To this girl that woman was the best cook, singer, and explainer ever. To curl up in Jenny's arms was very reassuring and was a spot that was always available. Jenny was her best friend in all the world, and that world was a special place known only to a few. Jenny had worked for the O'Malley family for twenty years and would continue on for twenty more, in her words, "If God's willin' and the river don't rise."

It was the combination of Jenny and her salt pork that brought forth the day's blessings from the kitchen. Anyone who had eaten from that kitchen would agree that Jenny was the best cook in the whole world. Saturday's fare included pork and fried apples served with a sizeable pot of red beans. The only thing left to wish for was a skillet of corn bread, which was already in the oven of the old iron stove. Jenny could have had a brand new stove but declined the modern conveniences of the 20th century, deeming them "unnecessary" and declaring, "What we have works fine." It was mostly that Scots-Irish blood in her veins; she was always careful about a penny.

Cate loved to be by the window in the kitchen, curled up in the old Windsor chair that Jenny was intending to re-glue. Cate loved to watch that woman prepare these feasts, Jenny's sweet face covered with beads of sweat, her red and yellow rag tied neatly around her newly permed hair. Her hands showed hard work, nothing soft and dainty there. Her expansive middle was neatly concealed under a floral apron with strings that barely reached to tie. Her large flat feet were wedged in the sturdy shoes she had repaired time and time again.

But it was the eyes that told her story, a story that Cate begged her to tell often. Neither did she tire of listening to Jenny's singing. Her songs were sad at times because they spoke about longing to see the valley, something like, "Oh Shenandoah, I long to see you." But Cate's favorites were a song about grace that was amazing and another about an old man that was really a river.

Jenny had a sister named Pearl Marie, but people just called her Pearl. Actually Jenny had a second name too. She was baptized Virginia Bird Drummond, after a famous actress that her mother had really admired. But she did not like her double name anymore than Cate did, so she had made it short and sweet, just Jenny. Names are important.

The sisters lived in the small cottage behind the garden. This was no ordinary garden, for in season it would bulge with onions, squash, beans, tomatoes, corn, potatoes, and every other vegetable the seed catalogue had to offer. Then there were the roses, Sweet William, daisies, and the tree peonies. The cottage was not ordinary either, with its gauzy window curtains and the painted furniture retrieved from the attic in the big house and the twin rockers settled next to their oversized radio. Jenny and Pearl spent most of their time in the big house with the O'Malleys, but this was indeed their own private place.

It was astonishing how different those two sisters looked; Jenny so stout; Pearl so stringy, boney, and weathered. They each had their own expertise, Jenny was inside with the house chores and cooking and Pearl was out in the garden with the beans and sweet peas. Pearl was ever so anxious for the weather to change to allow the turning of the dirt and the planting of her seeds. The sisters were both tough as leather and soft as down but that was about their heart and spirit, not their hands. You could hear their laughter from the kitchen and the garden. Added to their chores and selected pleasures, they had cared for their mother Edith Drummond until the year before the twins were born.

Their brother, Simus, had worked there at Kilhaven since he was thirteen years old and would be there until he joined his mother Edith in heaven. He had a comfortable room on the back side of the barn and mostly ate his meals with his sisters. The sisters and brother had been farm hands for hire. Simus had quit school at thirteen and was content to work the farm. They were happy there, very much a part of this family.

It was only natural for the O'Malleys to know everything about the background of this threesome that would become such an integral part of their lives; after all, this was the second generation of Drummonds to work on this property. They had an interesting heritage; they had lived by the Protestant ethic of hard work and good deeds. Their daddy, Patrick Hagan Drummond, had died young many years ago, but this family had been a part of the Scots-Irish settlement of the Shenandoah Valley since the Colonists had settled there in the early 1700s, with still a bit of that stern Presbyterian at their trunk.

When Cate was older she often begged Jenny in her typical loud shout, "Story, Jenny, Mama story! Jenny, Mama story." Cate loved to hear Jenny tell the story of her family. Jenny feigned resistance at first, then launched into the story as though it had never been told before.

"Well Cate, my mother's family came to Virginia from Pennsylvania and though some thought my mother, Edith, had enough Cherokee blood to live on a reservation, there was no real evidence of that. They claimed to be from somewhere in northwest Europe. They never had much money but they had a lot of pride. They were tough, salt of the earth folks, who could grow corn on a rock. They had never had a home or land of their own."

"I am proud of my family, especially my mother who deserves to be remembered. My mother, Edith, was from a large family and she loved to tell the story of standing with her mother and siblings waiting on a train platform with their trunks. A couple approached Edith's mother, my grandmother, and offered to buy one of the children. They said she was such a darling child, and they'd love to have her and, after all, it looked as if she had plenty more. Thankfully, my grandmother declined to sell." Jenny paused and Cate urged, "Books, Jenny. Tell the books."

"Well, we all took pride in a desire for education. That doesn't mean we all got one, but we desired it. My Aunt Patsy ran off with and married some man and had a baby. He loved Aunt Patsy dearly, and when he got money, he bought a set of encyclopedias and read them from beginning to end. He sent all three of his girls to school. They were good Presbyterians and they loved education!" Simus came in from the garden and Jenny, distracted, said, "That's enough, Cate. That's enough about my folks. I've got work to do."

Chapter Three

Any given morning would find Jenny already up with things simmering in the kitchen. She would vocalize in preparation to sing "Amazing Grace," especially on a Sunday, while preparing enough breakfast for everyone in the valley. As was the custom, leftovers would stay on the kitchen table under a cloth to be eaten at a later time during the day; an old farming tradition. The biscuits, butter, and jelly would complement the ham and with cold milk combine to make a most appreciated supper.

The tables were set for four in the kitchen and four in the dining room. It had been years since Cate had eaten anywhere but the kitchen because she chose to be with Jenny. She was happy there. Long ago, the dining room foursome had given up trying to convince her to eat with them. It was just not worth the chaos. Her screaming tantrums were just so hard to resolve.

The mahogany dining room table could be extended to seat twelve, but it had been a long time since it had hosted so many. Most days it was just Grandmother Grace O'Malley, Grandfather Michael O'Malley, Sr., brother Sean, and his and Cate's mother, Anna Lee Burke O'Malley, known as Neely. The table with the crisp white linen cloth sat squarely in the middle of the room under the brass chandelier that had been purchased by Grace and Michael when they had finally been able to buy this old home on land of their own.

Captivated by the beauty of this Virginia valley, the O'Malleys felt the happiness of a dream fulfilled. To honor their own Irish immigrant parents, they had christened the property, Kilhaven. It brought back memories of the villages in Ireland they had visited. Kilhaven gave the O'Malleys a sense of place and became the foundation of the O'Malley family. Situated in an extended cluster of oak, pine, maple, and tulip trees, one could still scan the horizon, so beautifully punctuated by a lake, a stream, and a ribbon of fencing that seemed to be purposefully guarding and protecting those who lived within its borders.

Kilhaven was particularly beautiful in the autumn. It was everyone's favorite time of the year. Cate especially loved the reds and yellows, and this showed in her art. It was a time when everyone looked forward to hearing Jenny say to her sister, "Pearl you need to start bringin' in the goods from the garden, so I can start my cannin.'"

On Sundays, Jenny, Pearl, and Simus made their way to early Sunday School at the Oak Hill Presbyterian Church. They went early so that they could get back home before the O'Malleys. Simus was a worrier and often said, "We best get on home 'fore the O'Malleys get there."

The O'Malleys faithfully attended Saint Patrick's Catholic Church in the village. They preferred the five o'clock mass on Saturday but often went to the Sunday service as well. They came in the front door after church, and they could smell the aromas coming from the kitchen. The dining table was set with the Sunday china.

On special occasions, Father Ryan Fleming from Saint Patrick's was invited to join the family for that main Sunday meal, especially at Easter when he was coming from a busy season of anointing and decorating and stripping the altar according to the various liturgical demands of that worship service. Jenny and Pearl once heard Father Fleming say that after Maundy Thursday he had "stripped the altar" for the Good Friday vigil. To them that was very strange. With their Presbyterian ways, the altar was always stripped, or at least it was not fancy. They preferred it that way. The plainer the better.

Father Fleming had been at Saint Patrick's for a long time. He boasted about the good works of his Altar Guild but loved to tell the story about one Saturday when one of the dear ladies poured out the water he had brought back from the Sea of Galilee. He had been saving it for years for some special event, he wasn't sure what, but he did take pleasure from knowing it was there. The family respectfully listened to the tale once again.

Father Fleming had a real relationship with this family having been through their most difficult times. He was always remembered and honored. Jenny would say, "This is good enough for Father Fleming!" She would admit to secretly being a little puzzled about the need for a white collar and was especially in awe of the long black veils on the Sisters at Saint Patrick's, but any reservations she had were discreetly concealed under a smile as she served her meals with great pride.

If it was the season for apple pie to be on the table, it would have been made from apples so abundantly provided by the orchard planted many years ago by Michael O'Malley, Sr. Grace would pitch in and become Jenny's assistant. Grace knew how to "put up" the canned goods, but when it came to the kitchen, Jenny was in charge and everyone knew it. Besides, Grace's memory slipped at times.

But all would agree that the most powerful relationship in that house was that of Cate and Jenny, who in combination provided the centrifuge of energy in every room. Their relationship was like leaping frogs, ever ready to jump in and heal the wound or share the joy. "We've been joined at the hip since the day she was born," Jenny claimed.

Putting aside that old adage, Cate's real experience with a near joining of the hips had been prenatal during her nine months of gestation. Then after the ordeal of birth, she learned that there really had been someone with her from the very beginning and that someone had now grown into a tall handsome boy of nine years who had been given the name Sean Michael O'Malley III, her twin brother.

Chapter Four

There was no reason that Cate should or could have remembered her great-grandparents. John and Masie O'Malley had left the old world of Ireland in early 1922. After a difficult decision, they packed their bags with all they could selectively bring on a crowded ship, said good bye to loved ones, and sailed on the *Eastern Guide* to the not so open arms of Ellis Island. The confusion, the crowded conditions, and the immigrants who were ill from the long trip met the O'Malleys head on. Since 1917, laws required immigrants to prove themselves with a literacy test. They were frightened beyond measure to be tested in this new country knowing that failure would mean certain return to Ireland. But they passed the test and made their way to New York.

Though they had missed that wretched potato famine in the mid-1800s, some seventy-eight years later there were still plenty of problems related to poverty, religion, and war that were always off and on. They sought a new life and believed the stories of promise and profit that were possible in America. It helped to have relatives that had gone before.

Ultimately settling in Jersey City, New Jersey, they began their new life. By 1924 their first son, Sean Michael, was born. They called him Michael. John and Masie devoted themselves to hard work and making a good life providing for their son and later their three other children.

John O'Malley must have had a four leaf clover stuck in his worn pocket as he just happened to be in the right place at the right time. Michael's father had opened a small grocery, then a bar, and both were immensely successful. O'Malley's Grocery and O'Malley's Tavern grew and provided John and Masie a way out of the ghetto and eventually a means to acquire more and more property. They did well, and they made it possible for Michael and his siblings to go to college.

Michael met the love of his life, Grace Rose Calagan, at Saint Paul's Catholic Church in Jersey City, and feeling an instant attraction too strong to ignore, they married three months later. Michael was tall, handsome, and ethical. He was determined to help with the expenses of his education and had worked throughout the four years of college. He graduated with honors and soon started an engineering company, which was successful. He was a fair man, providing for his workers with respect and reward for service.

Michael's personality embraced all the qualities that would make him the strong patriarch he became. He was steady, considerate, and kind. Michael was a reader at Saint Paul's Church, and he established a day care center in the church basement.

Michael's bride bore her name perfectly as she was lovely, kind, and full of grace. Michael thought she was beautiful, and she truly was beautiful. She graciously served as the church organist and faithfully visited the sick. Later, they filled those roles at Saint Patrick's.

Michael and Grace had completed their studies when they met. He had studied engineering and agriculture, and she studied languages and business. Grace had taught French in a private high school for enough years to save for their future home.

They were frugal people who had a dream of their own farm and their combined inheritance and savings made it possible to buy the land that would become the homestead of the O'Malleys, both present and future. They had looked long and hard for what they imagined would be their home for themselves and future generations. A short business trip had convinced them that Virginia was where they wanted to be. They had chosen the beautiful Shenandoah Valley.

Michael and Grace never imagined that they would have sadness equal to their joy. But they were practical people who had lived long enough to know that life was an uneven mix of highs and lows, and at times pure frustration. The early deaths of both their parents was seen as a loss they could hardly bare. The sadness they felt was to last for the rest of their lives.

After years of trying, the birth of their son Sean Michael O'Malley, Jr., enriched their marriage. They would have had a large Irish Catholic family but that was not to be so they counted their blessings in having that one son. They had the joy of raising him at Kilhaven, and they enrolled him in Millford, a nearby private school in Haily, Virginia. This was to prepare him for college. They watched him thrive and excel in college and then join his father in the engineering business. They saw him fall in love and marry.

Sean Michael, as they preferred to call him, was a good son in every way. He was grateful to his parents for the life they provided and would find ways to acknowledge this throughout his life. So, it was the darkest moment of their lives when an accident of the most devastating nature took him from them. It was a misbegotten attempt to move the stump of a tree with a very old tractor. Sean Michael's father had intended to replace that old tractor for some time and urged his son to wait. But it was not something that could wait. The huge old stump was squarely in the way of a greenhouse that was to be built for Grace and for her they would do anything at anytime.

During a weekend visit, Sean Michael was up early and after eating his usual favorite farmer's breakfast of pancakes and sausage, he donned his old overalls that hung on a hook in the mud room. He gave his pregnant wife Neely, a hug and dashed off to the barn to crank up the old John Deere. At first it failed to start, and it would have been a blessing in disguise if Sean Michael had not persisted in order to hear that sound of the fussy old engine. But persist he did, and soon he was on his way out of the barn and to the back yard where there would soon be a new glass home for Grace's roses.

The clanking of the old tractor motor was a nuisance, but it was somewhat reassuring for those listening in the house— at least to know that it was working. It was the loud terrifying crash and sudden silence that served as a signal that something was terribly wrong. It was Simus who ran from the barn only to see the wheels of the tractor still spinning, the tractor on its side and Sean Michael underneath. He head was severely injured and Simus could see that he had to move him.

Simus began to yell for help but knew that he had to get Sean Michael out from under that tractor as soon as possible. The turning wheels made that difficult for Simus. The tractor had rooted out the stump, which was catapulted into the air in pieces, coming down on Sean Michael. Unfortunately, the process had also caused the tractor to overturn onto Sean Michael. It was with an adrenaline driven unimaginable strength that Simus managed to move the heavy vehicle and pull Sean Michael out from under. Sean Michael was critically injured when the stump hit his head.

An ambulance to a CareFlight helicopter to the nearby city was followed by Grace, Michael, and Neely. They arrived at the hospital only to learn that Sean Michael was in surgery. He did not survive, living only an hour after surgery. Their sad and shocking goodbyes were said in the intensive care unit.

The disbelief, shock, and grief that permeated Kilhaven following his death was almost unbearable. Their grief was deeply shared by the dedicated Drummond family who had dutifully worked for this family for so many years and had watched Sean Michael grow up. These good Presbyterians had never been inside a Catholic Church and most certainly never been to a mass but they sat with the family at the service.

After the funeral mass at Saint Patrick's, Sean Michael was buried in the nearby village cemetery dedicated to Southern heroes. Sean Michael was to be their future when he died at the age of only twenty-five, but he gave them Neely, his young wife, pregnant with twins.

Neely was completely devastated by the loss of Sean Michael, so with nowhere to turn, she made Kilhaven her home. It was a time when most families would bond together and in the eye of this agonizing storm, Michael and Grace embraced Neely with a real love they had for a new daughter. With broken hearts, they faced an uncertain future with challenges unimaginable.

After the funeral mass at Saint Patrick's, Sean Michael was buried in the nearby village cemetery dedicated to Southern heroes. Sean Michael was to be their future when he died at the age of only twenty-five, but he gave them Neely his young wife pregnant with twins.

Neely was completely devastated by the loss of Sean Michael, so with nowhere to turn, she made Killhaven her home. It was a time when most families would bond together and in the eve of this agonizing storm, Michael and Grace embraced Neely with a real love they had for a new daughter. With broken hearts, they faced an uncertain future with challenges unimaginable.

Chapter Five

S ix weeks passed ever so slowly, and Neely sat in the swing on the front porch. Moving back and forth in front of the parlor windows she could see herself swaying in the glass. The old glass panes made her look distorted and that is just how she would have described herself. Distorted and dizzy with grief, she allowed her thoughts to wander back to the time when she had fallen so completely in love with Sean Michael.

Having met Sean Michael her sophomore year in college, she knew from the beginning that they would make a life together. They were very much in love. They had fun those years with only the cares and worries of final exams. At graduation Neely had been bold enough to tell her parents, a very traditional Virginia family, "I am going to marry Sean Michael O'Malley, Jr." From past exchanges, Neely had a hint of what their reaction might be and decided emphatically against Sean Michael going to ask her father for permission. Her instincts had proven correct.

The reaction of Mr. and Mrs. Burke came in a rage that was jarring; in a loud adamant roar, her father declared, "No daughter of ours will ever marry a Catholic! We do not believe as they do. They worship the Pope and they confess their sins to a priest! What about God?"

The crazy thinking! Their unfounded volatile objections were rooted in a curious narrow obsolescence. Neely did not share the view of her parents nor could she understand the fallacy of their misconceptions that basically believed that their religion was the only path to worship and to an afterlife in heaven. Even still, in determined exclamations, these devoted members of the Independent Church of Life vowed, "We forbid you to do this."

Neely fully expected that this harsh and extreme response would soften with time. She was wrong, but she was a determined young woman and she was in love. With all the courage within her, she informed them that she would marry Sean Michael and she did. The O'Malleys tried to fill in the void brought about by the absence of the Burkes at the small wedding at Kilhaven. They had learned that, in more ways than one, they truly had a new daughter.

Like his father, Sean Michael had been an educated man and also like his father, a person who had immense pride in his heritage. His loyalty to his family had been both admirable and intense. His engineering future had held great promise. He also loved to spend time moving the earth at Kilhaven where he had grown up loving the land. He was devoted to his parents, and though he and Neely lived nearby, they spent most weekends and holidays at Kilhaven. He was mindful of their needs, and he and Neely took them back to Ireland for a visit with their relatives and their roots. They visited many of the O'Malleys who had stayed in the Old World. They went to pubs, toured the village of their ancestors, and reinvested themselves in each other.

Sean Michael and Neely found their greatest joy at Kilhaven. They loved to swim in the pond and join in the harvesting in the fall. It was not unusual for Sean Michael to help with special projects at the farm. Sean Michael had volunteered to remove that stump. It was his intense love of being at Kilhaven that had so unexpectedly and sorrowfully ended his life.

Even in tragedy, Neely's parents had been aloof, objecting to the complicated tradition of the Catholic rituals of funeral. They did not attend the mass. Hurt was added to hurt and the gap grew wider. Before the wedding Neely had been confirmed in the Catholic Church, and when they heard of it, they renounced her and her decision. It was after her parents' refusal to come to Sean Michael's funeral that Neely chose, once and forever, to be an O'Malley and remain with his family at Kilhaven. Neely sobbed when she told Grace that her parents let her go with no plans to see her again.

Chapter Six

S o it was that Kilhaven and all who lived inside its fences prepared themselves for the birth of twins. Jenny and Pearl were in a state of combined grief, worry, excitement, and apprehension. In their spare time, they threw themselves into knitting and tatting, planning for at least one girl.

Neely spent the next six months in a fog. She had lost her husband, she was expecting twins, she had been rejected by her parents, and she had moved to a new home. The grief she bore consumed her. It was a grief so intense that it had the power to trump the joy she might have known with the anticipation of becoming a mother. She took long walks, often with Simus who watched out for her making sure she was safe. Awkward and unsophisticated, still Simus was like a brother to her. She could trust his friendship, and wanting to become more fully a part of Kilhaven, she asked Simus many questions. The answers she received began the creation of an understanding that would last long after some family members were gone. She naturally gravitated to Jenny and Pearl as their love was so graciously offered and easy to accept.

Feeling it was a some kind of warning, Neely told Grace of a recurring dream she was having that bothered her greatly. She described imagining hiking along a mountain path and losing her footing and tumbling into white water below. She had the sensation of drowning. She experienced daydreams as well, and in those she had a foreboding sense that something would not be ok for at least one of the babies. She had originally planned to give birth to the babies at home, but with these uncomfortable premonitions, she decided to go to Saint Vincent's Hospital in the city where they had the latest high-tech medical machinery. It turned out to be a critically important decision that would ultimately save her life.

Perhaps it was a time when ruminating or reminiscing was easy to come by, but in her free association with Grace she remembered when she was only eight years old, she told her best friend that she was certain she would one day have twins. She felt she would have two girls. When learning she would indeed have twins, she was told one was a girl and the other was uncertain. Later when she learned the other was a boy, she was surprised, but felt that she had been expecting that little girl for twenty years. Later in life, Neely would say that she felt that Cate had been with her since she was eight years old.

Those were days when Neely and Grace became very close and would develop a bond that would see them through more troubles. Grace loved to do little things for Neely. Grace never having had a daughter of her own, and Neely filled that void. For Neely, Grace became the mother that she never had. Even when she was in the good graces of the Burkes, she did not feel a real connection. She had longed for someone who was warm and affectionate and was willing to let herself be loved in return for the love she was willing to give.

Grace was with Neely through all the discomfort and preparation, throughout her pregnancy. With her due date five weeks away, Neely was still taking walks with Simus. This day, they walked even though Neely wasn't feeling well. Her back ached and she thought she felt something different, which was soon to become pain. About half an hour of walking was all she could do. She turned to Simus and said, "I really think it is time to go."

Simus was anxious. Grandfather O'Malley had planned to take Neely to the hospital when her time came, but he was away buying cattle on this day. In his absence, Simus volunteered to take his place leaving Grace free to watch after Neely. Though

Simus was a good driver, his nerves were sitting on his shoulder as he thought of the responsibility of getting her to the hospital in time. With Grace and Neely in the back, this anxious trio set out to drive into the city to Saint Vincent's Hospital for the birth of her babies. Grace held Neely's hand and timed her contractions. Neely was understandably frightened, and she wished for Sean Michael as all the uneasy moments of her pregnancy resurfaced.

There had been some indications that things were not right throughout the pregnancy. Jenny had sufficient midwife instincts to think so. It seemed as if one of the babies was always in the same location quietly sleeping with few indications of movement, while the other was always shifting and turning and kicking. A sonogram held the clue of a sleepy, quiet boy and a rambunctious, restless girl.

At the hospital a kindly nurse met them at the sliding doors with a wheelchair and that was the last thing Neely knew until she awoke with two cribs by her bed, each holding a tiny newborn. She found out that during her unconscious state, she had been taken for an emergency caesarean section when the medical team discovered pre-eclampsia, which was causing her kidneys and liver to fail. While Neely's life was in jeopardy, Grace O'Malley paced the floor of the waiting room and sent Simus home to retrieve Jenny and Pearl just for moral support. It was no time to be alone. She prayed to herself that they would not be faced with yet another tragedy.

Grace's prayers were heard. Neely delivered her twins, a boy and a girl. It was 1982 the same year as the birth of Prince William in England. The twins were healthy, each with sufficient weight and breathing on their own. Within the week following, they were released from the hospital and Jenny and Pearl each carried out one baby for their first trip to Kilhaven. The bundles were small, one in a pink blanket, the other one in blue so lovingly knitted by these dear old nannies. The first sight of Mary Caitlin and Sean Michael O'Malley III, would have likely touched anyone who saw these two little ones who came into the world fatherless. So it was Grandfather O'Malley who excitedly met them at the door with a bouquet of roses for Neely.

Cate had red hair, appropriate as it was to become her favorite color. Red allowed her to express herself as needed and she used it often. Sean had blonde hair that looked like it might be curly. With beautiful skin and bluish eyes, they were understandably the center of attention. They were also to be the saving grace of a family in full resolve to pick up the pieces, to try to diffuse their grief and to focus on this double blessing of new life.

Chapter Seven

Neely attempted to nurse her babies two at a time, but it soon became clear that she was not up to the task. Jenny and Pearl took over and with the two of them working around the clock, it was almost too much, even for them. In addition to the chores of floors to mop and meals to prepare, they now prepared the bottles and fed the babies.

Rocking the baby girl, Jenny was the first to realize there was something different about Cate. The prenatal behaviors were too obviously continued with a serene happy baby boy and a flailing, screaming, restless baby girl.

Grace was feeling overwhelmed. "I don't want to say it Jenny, but I just have a feeling that something is wrong with Cate," she sighed.

Neely, trying hard to overcome a depression resulting from death and now exacerbated by birth, was struggling to do the routine, not the extraordinary, but even in her disheartened confusion, she agreed with both Jenny and Grace.

They stood together trying to decipher the meaning behind the cries of the baby girl that daily lasted for hours at a time. During those trying hours, it took everyone in the house to join in and help. Cate had severe colic and could go for hours without sleep. It was in those first months they came to dread the full moon, as that seemed to make matters worse. Jenny declared, "On those nights with a full moon my baby girl is totally upset." She believed in home remedies and insisted that the babies had to always wear socks even in the hot summer, and once in a while she was known to give that baby girl some water with a tiny drop of whiskey. This actually helped, but she had to use it sparingly. Those who were there to provide care were at times desperate but nothing helped for long. At least both babies were healthy and even chubby.

At four months, Jenny thought some fresh air and sunshine would be a good thing for her most unhappy little girl. She said, "Catie girl, I will just bundle you up and take you out to the sunshine." They went outside near the garden and Cate instantly became agitated in the extreme. The sun seemed to terrify her. She was shaking and crying and so disturbed that Jenny immediately took her inside.

Cuddling the little body to her breast she wondered, "My darlin' girl, how can you hate the sunshine? Everybody loves the sun." As she comforted Cate, she wondered why she could not seem to get her attention: Cate simply looked away, focused on nothing.

Sean was behind Cate in development. At six months she was the first to roll over, she was also the first to crawl, and by nine months she could walk. Sean did not walk until four months later. By the time Cate was twelve months old, everyone in the house had recognized her temper, which often caused her to bang her head against the wall or her bed. She was obsessed with wanting to carry things and took a definite interest in colored markers, the plastic sort with a top. She only wanted blue markers and was happy just to walk around carrying several blue markers in her hand. She never attempted to use them; she simply wanted to carry them. Then she decided to carry spoons.

Jenny said, "This child has some mighty strange ways," but in spite of the difficulties, Cate was indeed Jenny's girl. She recognized that Cate's anger was most intense when she could not have what she wanted. While that was not unusual for children, every reaction from Cate was extreme and tantrums were a part of every day.

By the time the babies were a year old, the difference in their development could not be denied. The household had soon realized that in Cate there was a behavior they had to try to understand. She had developed faster than her brother but it was a frenetic development. It was at this time that Neely stumbled on an article in a book describing some of the indications of autism. There were so many similarities in the description and Cate's behavior that Neely began to worry, mostly from just not knowing what it was or what to expect or what could be done. These worries grew.

Neely now began her serious but uneasy journey with Cate through the medical profession. After the initial examination, the first of many doctors said, "Autism…too young to tell, just watch it." Another doctor had the same response. "Too early to tell…just wait and see." In a sense, they were saying all they knew or that was known. So much was yet to be learned. Yet, the behaviors continued and increased as Cate had more experiences. Loud noises, bright lights, and food aromas all caused her to scream with anxiety.

When Cate was about eighteen months old she stopped smiling and stopped talking. She seemed to regress. Whereas she had used the words "ball" and "mama," she gave them up and didn't want to play anymore. She stopped looking at people. She started waking up in the middle of the night and would scream for hours. The pediatrician said, "Let's wait and see."

By the time she was two, she had chronic diarrhea and drooled uncontrollably. The doctor flatly dismissed it with "A lot of kids with autism have diarrhea." Nothing was to be done. Cate walked on her toes, flapped her hands, and spent much of the time starring into the middle distance. Neely and Grace went from one doctor to another hoping for an explanation and guidance.

When Cate was two and a half, the answer came in a most matter of fact manner: "Your child has autism. It is a genetic brain disorder. We are not sure what causes it and there is no cure. Forty hours a week of therapy might make her behavior more acceptable, but it's not going to 'cure' her. You need to start looking at institutions now because the good ones have long waiting lists."

The doctor sent Neely home with a video that was supposed to help, and she sobbed as she, Jenny, and Grace watched children like Cate rocking, flapping their hands, and screaming. The film narrator said, "We all have great dreams for our children. With the diagnosis of autism, the dream dies."

Neely was astounded. Therapy? Institutions? Waiting lists? What did this mean? She was barely able to walk from weakness that ran throughout her body. She was not ready for such conjecture. How could they say those things?

The staff at the Children's Center confirmed the diagnosis in most certain terms: "Mrs. O'Malley, as the parent of a child newly diagnosed with autism, you need to overcome the hope that there might be a thinking, conscious, emotionally-attuned child 'hidden' within her. You need to come to terms with the fact that all there is to Cate is on the surface. If she has something to say, she'll say it, her not talking means she has nothing to say... she is thinking and feeling nothing and there is no point to hope otherwise."

The morning after Cate's diagnosis, Neely woke up wondering in a disorganized but hopeful way that it had been a bad dream. Then sinking into the realization that the diagnosis was reality, the knot in her stomach once again took charge.

With such discouraging news, Neely wondered if the professionals were correct in their assessment and advice. How could they be so certain when everything about this disorder seemed so uncertain? Neely reasoned that Cate never seemed typical in her development, but she did answer to her name and she had been speaking to an extent.

Maybe amazing things could happen? Once in a while, some did happen. These were the little dribbles of hope that could make a difference. One early nightfall, Neely was taking Cate into the house, her little head nuzzled on Neely's shoulder. Though covered with a blanket, Cate peeked out from under it, then she pointed and said "up." Her eye had caught the moon and she knew that it was "up." Neely grabbed at any and all incidents that left the impression that Cate was grasping an understanding of her environment.

Neely would later describe her feelings of that moment. "I often felt that autism was gravity amplified … like Cate was being sucked into something that was beyond my reach." Every event brought a new message; some were encouraging, others not. But Neely would look back one day and acknowledge two major realizations in this journey.

First, she came to believe that mainstream medicine had totally failed them, before and after the diagnosis. Thinking back she felt a crushing sense of guilt that her child might have been all right if only she had not failed to ask a certain nurse whether the vaccine she was administering to Cate contained mercury, or perhaps the autism resulted from her not reminding a technician that she had failed to wash her hands. What was it? What brought this about? When did this start? Was it before or after she was born?

But the other reality for her was to acknowledge that no one knows what causes autism. Over time she discovered that many caregivers of autistic people object to the medicalization of the autism diagnosis. They understood those with autism as different, not deficient. Or that even if autism was the result of medical mistakes or environmental mishaps, those with autism were what they were, and they are fine in themselves. Neely felt that the disconnect was between their needs and the social environments in which they find themselves. Some feel that they just landed on the wrong planet.

It took years for Neely to release herself from all these doubts and fears and guilt. She fortified herself with a resolve to somehow create a context in which Cate could enjoy being her own autistic self. She sought for Cate a little part of the earth where she could feel at home.

One night when the twins were almost three (six months after Cate's diagnosis), Neely realized how her mind was completely exhausted. She made her way out to Pearl's garden and sat down on a little stool used for planting. She looked up and was actually shocked by the night sky. She thought, "There are still stars?" She hadn't looked up in so long. The realization that nature still continued to exist took her by surprise.

Leaving the stars behind, Neely returned inside, still unable to sleep; she could not escape the enormity of her tasks. She returned to the parlor, opened the desk drawer, and retrieved a book that held poetry that had given her strength and direction. She had read it many times. Now she needed to read it again.

THROW YOURSELF LIKE SEED

Shake off this sadness, and recover your spirit:
Sluggish you will never see the wheel of fate
That brushes your heel as it turns going by,
The man who wants to live is the man in whom life is
    abundant.

Now, you are only giving food to that final pain
Which is slowly winding you in the nets of death
But to live is to work and the only thing which lasts
Is the work; start there, turn to the work.

Throw yourself like seed as you walk, and into your own
    field,
Don't turn your face for that would be to turn it to death
And do not let the past weigh down your motion

Leave what's alive in the furrow, what's dead in yourself,
For life does not move in the same way as a group of
    clouds:
From your work you will be able one day to gather
    yourself

—Miguel de Unamuno

A quiet knock on the door was followed by the timid voice of Simus. He limped in, his hat in hand and asked, "Is this a good time Miz Neely? I know it's late, I just finished puttin' up the chickens for the night but I feared you were troubled and I've been waitin' for a good time to show you somethin'." He continued, "It's out on the screened porch…somethin' I made for you."

He motioned for her to follow. "I was out in the woods one day and I saw this split log. It came to me on purpose I think, jes' so I could make somethin' for you."

Stepping out on the porch, Neely saw a beautiful little table. It was made from a huge tree that had fallen, its wide trunk had split into the shape of a heart.

Simus was not one to show his emotions, but on this night he looked at Neely with tears in his eyes and said, "This here's your broken heart."

She put her arms around his skinny neck and said, "Simus if ever I had a real blood brother, I would want it to be you. You are precious to me."

He blushed, smiled, tipped his hat, and very quietly bid her good night.

In time, Neely came to believe that the heart was not broken after all, it was cracked at the top but the center and point held. The heart was not ruined, it was simply made larger.

Chapter Eight

Wisdom did not come easily. Neely and the O'Malleys went through all the steps of grief, from denial to acceptance. In her confusion and despair, Neely often found her way to the old wicker rocking chair on the back porch. As she looked out over the meadow, she could begin to see the mountains and knew that soon they would be clearly visible. It was autumn again and it seemed to her that everything around her was dying, rather than just going to sleep for the winter. The real beauty of the bright yellow sugar maple escaped her and the blazing red oak's glow meant nothing. Grief was still with her and she was incapable of sorting through her situation or its implications. She actually had no idea what lay ahead. This she did know—things were not very good.

It seemed to her that she could never know enough about Cate's problems. Her need to know more was only natural. She finally opened one of the many books she had been given to read. It was daunting in its language and scientific underpinnings, and she closed the book. She went to the kitchen, leaving the rocker still rocking.

"I think I'd like a cup of hot tea," she told herself, and as she put the kettle on the stove, she realized she was just avoiding what had to be done. After all the doctors, all the waiting, all the wondering, she had to find answers on her own. She had to try to understand. She had been going through the motions, nodding and pretending to understand, but she did not.

It was a disturbing pattern of events that made her realize that it was time to find her way through this mystifying disorder. She had put forth every effort toward the care and feeding of her children, but as Simus was heard to say, "It's time to reckon."

Pouring the boiling water over the tea bag, she returned to the porch, the rocker, and the book.

Feeling very much alone, she called upstairs and asked Grace to come down and read with her. It seemed easier when shared. She had long ago read the basics. According to her *Oxford American English Dictionary* the word *autism* came from the Greek word *autos* meaning *self*. It is a pervasive disorder in children and so forth … etc. etc. etc. She had heard that much already.

Desperation had a grip on Neely, both in her desire to know more and to find ways to cope with so much that she could not understand or define. This was not the beginning of her reading, there was that frightening article that had started her thinking in the beginning, and she knew it would not be the end. She needed information. Grace joined her in her search.

Neely found that there was agreement only in the need to know more and that included the professionals in this specialty. The professionals were still learning too. It was acknowledged that the causes of autism had baffled researchers for years, but new findings she read were encouraging experts to redouble their efforts to hunt for possible genetic and environmental explanations. Despite progress in unlocking some of the mysteries of autism, scientists had simply confirmed that there were likely numerous genetic causes and predispositions. Pinpointing these links and how they work was exceedingly complex and could take years to unravel, let alone counteract. The triggers were what eluded science still.

Neely struggled to concentrate. She closed the book then she opened it again. The message was discouraging, but Grace encouraged her to continue. She picked up one book after another, finding similarities in each as they related to each other. From a multitude of sources Neely and Grace synthesized and concluded a series of statements that seemed to clarify for them the indications of autism.

They had experienced them first hand. Neely remembered the withdrawal of Cate. She remembered leaning over Cate with a toy and attempting to gain her attention only to be met with Cate's stare off into space. She confirmed from experience that the hallmark indication of autism is impaired social interaction. Even as a baby Cate was unresponsive to people and seemed to focus intently on one item to the exclusion of others for long periods of time.

It was obvious to Neely that another common sign of autism is difficulty with verbal and nonverbal communication. She would test Cate by approaching her. "Cate, let's sing a song," she would say. Cate often failed to respond to her name and often avoided eye contact with other people. Clearly Cate was having difficulty interpreting what others were thinking or feeling because she could not understand social cues, and was not looking for clues about appropriate behavior.

Neely paused with information swirling in her head. She turned to Grace with a silent stare. It was clear that they both recognized all of these indications too well.

Cate expressed all of the major signs of autism which included repetitive movements, such as rocking or twirling, or self-abusive behavior such as biting or head banging. Neely could remember how she felt the first time she looked in while Cate sat on the floor rocking. She could remember Cate sitting quietly, never looking at her mother, trying to avoid the light and then often screaming from the smells of foods cooking in the kitchen.

Other indications, which Neely recognized along with social withdrawal, lack of eye contact, delayed language, loss of speech, and hand flapping, were hypersalivation, sleep difficulties, gastrointestinal disorders, preoccupation with certain objects or subjects, rituals, anxiety, irrational fears, and head banging. The head banging was particularly alarming to Grace and

Neely, especially when it was a reaction caused by anger. These instances were so much harder to bring back to a calm.

Neely sought studies of autistic twins and learned that the chances of both twins becoming autistic were much lower for fraternal twins, than that of identical twins. Since Cate and Sean were fraternal twins, there was some relief in that knowledge, but the thought of both children being autistic, was too much to consider. Though there had been no indication of autism in Sean, it was a thought that was more than Neely could bear.

Neely told Grace, "I suppose once the unimaginable has happened to you, you feel vulnerable to it happening again. None of us are guaranteed that it will not happen again."

Grace could see the fear in Neely's eyes. Grace reached over to hug Neely and then closed the book. The thought was overwhelming. To think that it could happen to both her children was too much for one day. Neely turned to Grace and said, "It's time to feed the twins." The two of them made their way to the kitchen for the thrice daily challenge of feeding the children.

Chapter Nine

W hen Cate was four years old, she again began to say words. She had a sufficient vocabulary but preferred to try and get what she wanted by using only one word. She had to be coaxed, which was actually a form of creating a response with a reward for changed behavior. Her inclination was to repeat words and actions, which made this form of training a natural for her. Neely would coax her with the word "on" to get the radio to play. Each time the word "on" was spoken the radio would be turned on for her to hear. One day she made the connection between performance and response. She eventually added "radio" to her vocabulary, and when used with the word "on," she could get what she wanted.

It was during this period that Neely realized the need for some major training to get Cate out of diapers. Sean had been trained at the age of two, but Cate was very comfortable with the way things were and was not eager for change. She had resisted so violently in the past that Neely knew that this would likely be one of the more difficult of all their learning experiences.

Neely pulled up a stool with Cate on the potty and began the arduous task of showing this same "performance/response" or "positive reinforcement" routine in the new setting of the green tile bathroom. Of course neither of them wanted to spend that much time in the green tile bathroom, but for four long days, the two of them kept their seats waiting for Cate to make the connection between desired behavior and the reward of a jelly bean.

They talked, they read stories, they colored, and drew pictures. The tedium of the effort was beyond description for each of them. At times, Cate would try to leave, she would scream, rock, bang her head, and even bite her arm. Bringing her back was an act of force for Neely. By the end of each day they were both exhausted and discouraged.

On the fourth day, the connection was made. The behavior was rewarded and the light came on in Cate's head. A major hurdle had been conquered, and it was cause for celebration at Kilhaven.

Grandfather O'Malley also spent many hours with Cate. They each had their own comfortable chair for their movies and spent hours watching the same film over and over. He was very patient, and though he had seen favorites many times, he watched them again and again with her.

Grandfather O'Malley was fascinated with this beautiful child. One could never predict what she might do or say, and that was in some ways compelling. When she smiled it was as if nothing was different. Her shiny red hair was the same color as her father's, and Grandfather O'Malley loved to pat her on the head and recall the times when his own little son would put his red head on his dad's shoulder. He never gave up on trying to understand. Even when he did not, he endured.

The more abstract challenges were not so easily defined but in doing so, little mysteries were revealed. When she was five, Cate became obsessed with the story of Pinocchio. Grandfather read that book to her over and over. She seemed to identify with Pinocchio. She began to ask questions, "Me in cage? Whale swallow me? Me real girl? You Blue Fairy?"

Although clearly drawn to fantasy, she was also perhaps seeking reassurance that she was safe and needed to know there was someone there to protect her. Or perhaps she could identify with the troublesome marionette who could never seem to get anything right. Grandfather O'Malley was never sure how to answer her questions, but he did his best to reassure her. "No, Cate, you will not be put in a cage. You will not be swallowed by a whale. I will be your Blue Fairy. You are already a real girl and you are safe," he reassured her. She loved what he had to say, and his reward was her hugs and smiles.

It was difficult to unravel each new puzzle, but the family was learning. Neely was astounded when she began to realize that Cate was learning to speak by listening to the words she heard. For this reason, movies were even more important for their sounds. Movies were added to color and art as essential elements of her language.

The family began to see that for Cate to learn, it was essential for her to embrace a particular interest. They believed that in finding that interest they could perhaps find Cate hiding in there and get a glimpse of her underlying capacities. She might not be able to speak in her own voice, but she could speak through the voice of a cartoon character that she impersonated. In using that voice she could possibly begin a conversation that would go beyond the cartoon context. This could be the most important breakthrough possible.

Cate also became infatuated with *Alice in Wonderland*. She would watch it, run it to a point…pause…rewind…play it again…rewind…play it again. Perhaps she could identify with the fantasy world, the peculiar anthropomorphic creatures, and the riddles. It became obvious that Cate, even with her developmental disabilities, could "echo" what she heard. Cate may not have known what the words meant, or maybe she did. She made a connection, which was hopeful even if she was just repeating the last sound. Most adults assumed that autistic children do not know what the words mean, but Neely felt that perhaps there was a meaning, logic, and connection; and that these could be found if one were patient, sensitive, open-minded, and smart enough about the process.

As Cate sat in her little chair watching movies, she seemed comfortable. It was her parallel universe and where she found her way in expressing herself. Through movies she was exposed to a wider world. Movies joined her most treasured possessions along with her colors and her markers. Through mimicking and echoing, Cate was acquiring sounds and rhythms. Through her movies and art she could express herself.

Chapter Ten

At the age of five, Sean and Cate were enrolled in separate schools. Cate needed special education class and a place less demanding. She needed someone who had a clear understanding of autism. Her loud way of speaking her words, her lack of sensitivity to others, her angry tantrums were most disturbing, making it difficult to learn and certainly to establish relationships. Some parents complained about her behavior.

Sean was extremely bright, most popular with his classmates, and excellent student and a happy child. At home he was helpful and responsible, but he had ambivalent feelings toward his sister. He was protective in the sense that he did not tolerate anyone speaking ill of her, yet she was a real thorn in his side. She was loud and hyper with little, if any, consideration for the wants and needs of others. His defense was to isolate himself, closing himself off in his room. Neely made him a sign to put on his door that said, "Do Not Disturb." He was protective of his own things and was frustrated and angry when Cate slipped in one day and drew with markers on his wall. He wanted to yell at her and tell her to go away. She could be very destructive and he was embarrassed for his friends to see one of her fits or tantrums.

Cate had many quirks. She refused to wear shoes. She withdrew from strangers, preferring to be with those people she knew well. She was in a self-imposed isolation much of the time. It was Grandmother O'Malley who was the first to recognize that Cate's isolation must end in order that she could begin to learn. Grace O'Malley's training in languages was most helpful, and she was devoted to helping Cate in her attempts to communicate and develop some social skills. She observed the therapists who worked with Cate and applied her knowledge to theirs. Her tireless efforts in helping Cate were driven by her love for her; even when Cate refused to respond, her grandmother endured with kindness. These children were the remaining vestiges of her only son. There were layers of love that joined this grandmother and this little girl.

Cate loved her grandmother very much. It was not unusual for Cate to beg to go for drives with her. Cate's favorite thing to do was spread one of Grace's handmade quilts in the meadow and have a picnic. Grace told Cate about the origin of each scrap, whose dress that had been. "I wore that pretty blue silk for my sixteenth birthday party, and you will have one when you are sixteen." Cate wasn't sure about what that meant, but she loved the blue silk.

Grace told her how the quilt was made from a frame hanging from the ceiling. "I remember crawling under the frame when it had a quilt on it, and I would hide from my grandmother," Grace would recall. They made up stories and played games on the fabrics of checks and plaids. They would laugh and decide which ones they liked the best. Then Cate would gleefully draw a picture of the quilt on her paper with her many markers. She never tired of this experience and wanted to do the same thing all over again and again.

Everyone in that house had learned something about being with Cate, but it was Grandmother O'Malley who taught her a few words in French and granted her special privileges. Cate's favorite was to go through an old jewelry case just loaded with jewels and memories. Cate's favorite piece was an old cameo, worn so many years ago by Grace's own grandmother. When Cate managed to say the lovely French words, Grace would reward her by allowing her to wear the old cameo.

"Bone shure," Cate would say with pride and all she really knew was that it pleased her grandmother and that was all she really cared about at those times.

Cate's ability to love was most visible in a smile or a hug. The ugliness of the angry and frustrated behaviors was balanced by her expressions of affection and those instances helped put aside some of the stress.

By the age of seven there was considerable change. She was not only under the care of a physician and a speech therapist, but she had been referred to Miss Ava Rankin, an art teacher with great patience. Miss Rankin opened many doors for the obstreperous but precocious little girl who was attempting to communicate in her own ways. Often those ways were not so agreeable. But Miss Ava seemed to have been sent from some special place of understanding. Through color, she brought a new way of helping Cate and color helped link her to the larger world.

Cate had long since acquired her own paper and paints. She loved to make intricate pictures, but when painting, Cate could not be interrupted without severe repercussions. No two tasks could be done at the same time. No two senses could be called upon simultaneously.

Her need to repeat all behaviors or words was accompanied by a need to put them on paper in color. Miss Ava seemed to have a unique understanding that this child needed to be comfortable with her difference, not to try to make her more "normal." This WAS her "normal" and it likely always would be thus.

In her search for meaningful ways to teach Cate, Miss Ava found the garden to be the answer. Her studio itself was an inspiration, painted a soft pewter blue with a mustard color door and shutters. Miss Ava was what the neighbors referred to as a "spinster lady." She was tall and a bit gangly, with beautiful hands and long fingers that wrapped around a paint brush with an elegance that felt like velvet, but her real beauty was in her calm demeanor with Cate. That came from a true love for the child and a desire to encourage her growth, with the hope of creating a world in which she could be comfortable.

It was in the garden that they had their adventures in color and how color could express one's feelings. Miss Ava would ask Cate to find a color in the flowers that would demonstrate a feeling such as "happy." Cate would look carefully at all possibilities and choose a tall white daisy with a yellow center. Cate would then paint the daisy. Miss Ava would then challenge Cate to find something soft, which led her to a patch of beautiful gray foxglove. Then there was another painting. Red color seemed to represent anger or other strong emotions. Miss Ava sat quietly by while Cate would explore. There was always Cate's love for the iris.

Cate's many paintings were very private, in that she never wished to explain them or to be complimented about them. She would become very agitated if asked to explain her work. She would drive everyone away. If she was told that she was beautiful or smart or talented or a good artist, she would fly into a rage. She might then do a savage painting of reds and oranges and yellows that seemed to scream off the page. There was no mistaking it when she was angry. She might say, "I'm bad, I'm bad!" using the strong language she had borrowed from a recent movie.

Neely's way of responding to that rage was to remind her that she loved her. Cate would eventually grumble, then object with diminished vehemence, as if Neely's logic had gotten through to her. Once in a while, she would make a statement that did shed some very limited light on the meaning of her art, but she delivered it in such a way as to imply that anyone should know that certain colors express certain feelings. She would become angry at times if it seemed that the interested party did not understand.

Cate's creativity was in every way unique, and the act of creating made her happy. The paintings were comprised of bright colors, organized scribbles that had a structure and form. There were bodies with hands and feet and expressive faces.

There was movement in the figures. There were letters of the alphabet combined in eccentric forms. Wheels and numbers were favorites. At first glance, the images were vague, but given time and focus the themes became clear, not their meaning, but their form. The challenge with the art was in keeping it from appearing on the walls of the house.

Cate often wanted a playmate, and she wanted it to be Neely. They could often be seen outside playing catch. Over and over they would throw the ball, then Cate would decide to aim at a branch in the tree. Again and again she would throw the ball at a tree branch. Whatever they did was repeated until another idea popped into Cate's head. Neely was always patient and kind. Neely would become the hoop for the ball to go through, she would be the bridge to cross, she would be the hub of the wheel, all according to what Cate could envision and initiate.

Loud noises, bright lights, and certain food aromas were still unbearable to Cate and caused her to throw fits of screaming and running. Food remained a source of contention in other ways as well. Textures were a problem. They could not be mixed. Seasonings that could be seen, such as pepper, were called "bugs." Any food with bugs on it was immediately rejected. Any food with a sign of fat was discarded, yet Jenny soon learned that one thing that both children would eat was bacon, perhaps they did not recognize fat in its crispy form.

"We are going to have to get us a pig just to keep those children filled and happy," she would say. But for eggs? Cate only ate the yolk and Sean only ate the whites. That was one thing that worked. But food was an issue that never went away. The only answer was to keep it simple.

One person who understood the need for simplicity was Laura, a special teacher's aide assigned to Cate in her first grade special ed class. Neely was very grateful to have someone at the school who understood Cate.

Chapter Eleven

One Sunday Father Fleming came to share the O'Malley table. He knew from past Sundays there was a heavy atmosphere at Kilhaven. This day, as Jenny brought the pot roast to the buffet in the dining room, she caught the attention of the old priest, for after all these years, they had developed an understanding complete with its own set of signals. Jenny's behavior today let Father know that she had something on her mind.

When the apple pie was finally only a smudge on his plate, Father Fleming put down his napkin and made his way through the swinging doors to the kitchen. As he entered, he saw Jenny staring out the window. It was strange to see her that way because that woman was never, ever, still. She turned and Father Fleming noticed a most unusual and unexpected tear in her eye. For a moment they just looked at each other in silence, each wondering what the other might be thinking.

Finally Father spoke, "Jenny, I have only seen you cry one other time and that was at the cemetery. What has happened to bring you to this again?"

Jenny hardly knew what to say. Her heart and head were full of questions with no answers and for her this was unusual. She had always managed to find answers, but this was different. She spoke, "Father Fleming this ol' woman is past ignorance. I know how to cook and clean and kill a chicken by wringin' its neck. I can sew a shirt, knit a blanket, clean a fish, birth a baby, and bury the dead, but I don't know how to really truly help my little girl." Jenny looked into the priest's eyes, her own eyes filled with tears and time. "Tell me how to do this. How do I help my girl? Did the good Lord send us this child for a special reason?"

Father Fleming wished for wisdom at this moment as he too was without answers. What to say? "Jenny, my dear, you are indeed past ignorance. I pray that I may do justice to your questions. The Lord I embrace is not vindictive and does not strike us down to teach us a lesson. The God I love gives us opportunities to love one another in many different ways. Your love for that child will lead you to the epiphany you seek. Prayer never hurts and provides us a much needed quiet time to reflect and open ourselves to the possibilities. We are given intelligence to seek answers and there are many who spend their days attempting to unlock this mystery that has our little girl in its grip.

"We all have our unique challenges and you have been given this as a gift. A game to play, a song to sing, a picture to paint, a meal to prepare, and a desire to understand. It will come to you. Call upon your heritage of hardship and disappointment. Call upon the strength of your ancestors who bravely left the Old World and immigrated here to the valley to make a new home. Call upon what you know is possible and that is to love this child unconditionally. Let her be who she is. Trust yourself. Run to the meadow with Cate. Let her see autumn."

Chapter Twelve

Jenny felt better. She thought to herself, "I can see why they call him Father. I feel almost like a child just listening to what he had to say. I sure wish there was a simple solution; it is so complicated." Then she put her thoughts away and just did what Father advised. She told Cate to gather her paper and paints while she packed a lunch of bacon and egg yolks. They were both eager to walk in the meadow; to hear the soft quarter notes of the cowbells and then go to the orchard to paint and pick the apples.

Neely had just finished a session with Cate about animals and what they do for us. They spoke of the cow's milk to drink, the chicken's eggs to eat, and the sheep's wool to keep us warm. But Cate just wanted to leave with Jenny for their picnic; her attention had completely turned away. As the squeaky kitchen door slammed, Neely gravitated to the parlor, her favorite room.

This lovely room had never lost its old fashioned feel. The matching blue velvet chairs, each with its own footstool, offered a nest of reassurance and quiet. Neely came here when she really wanted to think. She looked around the room and realized that this place had truly become home to her. She appreciated the antique writing desk with its silver inkwells that had no ink and had long ago turned the writing over to a black ball point. She loved that this room had no overhead lighting, with only its china lamps offering a glow to the wide plank pine floors. The walls were carefully papered in an old floral pattern and the crewel work sofa had its original cover; only its horse hair cushions had been refilled with down. She was grateful for the oriental rugs, since the twins were known for spills and mud. Anyway, she could relax and reflect in this room.

There were two great gaps in her heart. She missed Sean Michael and she missed her family. Her parents' resolve was stubbornly enforced and they had made it clear that they might possibly tolerate her being an O'Malley, but never a Catholic. Still they made no move to see her or the children.

"How is it," she wondered, "that grown-up people could be so prejudiced, so intolerant, so narrow-minded that they would deny themselves the joy of a daughter and grandchildren, just for the sake of thinking they were right?"

Such thoughts were just too painful to consider that day. She would just put them away for now because she needed to tell the O'Malleys that she was going to need a good bit of money to follow the recommendations from the latest conference with a new doctor, Dr. Eva Brickman. This doctor seemed to know what she was talking about and having an autistic child herself, there was an added dimension to her own desire to understand and advise.

Dr. Brickman was the director of the Memorial Hospital's Wing for Special Needs Children. Neely had found her way to Dr. Brickman by desperately searching through the phone book. She knew the city, as it was where the twins had been born, and felt she could find her way easily. Her desperation was prompted after a particularly difficult day when Cate had taken the goldfish out of its bowl, squeezed it and left it on the table. It died, but Cate seemed to make no connection between the two events. Certainly there was no remorse or accountability.

That incident had frightened and disturbed Neely. In desperation, she had turned to the *Yellow Pages*. Later she acknowledged to herself there had been some desperate force that became an energy guiding her. Through that she had found Dr. Brickman.

Since she knew little about the Children's Wing at the hospital, she was comforted to read the plaque on the door that said, "Since 1849 this Memorial Hospital has been a vital means for protecting the well being of those most in need." She had read that sign and decided that if "in need" was the criteria for admittance, she felt she qualified and with that little knowledge she made an appointment to bring Cate in to see the doctor.

With time and another visit, Neely felt she had indeed found a true professional and was ready to put her confidence in that finding. This sense of trust was a completely new experience and she was grateful. Finally, here was a professional who really understood, one who had walked in her shoes.

Dr. Brickman had suggested homeschooling for Cate and that it be done by specialists who worked with autistic children. She understood the labyrinth they would go through to find a way that was appropriate for Cate. Each situation was unique. Neely was uncertain about homeschooling. Things had been rough at school for Cate since her Miss Laura's contract to help Cate in the classroom had not been renewed. Neely was interested in meeting the therapists. Perhaps she would change her mind after meeting them.

Chapter Thirteen

It was late autumn in 1988 and Cate was seven years old. An early snow had been predicted. Neely was hoping it would hold off until after Dr. Brickman's assistants came to Kilhaven to meet the family. Leeba Ashman and Anat Levy were anxious to meet their new young charge.

When the guests arrived, Cate obstinately refused to leave the kitchen unless Jenny came too; hence a rather disjointed and convoluted quartet was created. It consisted of two young therapists, a very large cook/housekeeper, and a very small girl with red hair. Cate reluctantly met the members of her new "team," but she was not immediately convinced of their value. Neely was not on the team but faded into the background to observe.

Attempting to break the ice, Leeba explained that her name in Yiddish means "beloved," and Anat followed, "My name in Yiddish means 'to sing.'" No one in that room was sure that Cate understood, but Jenny concluded that "to sing" and "beloved" sounded pleasant enough and she thought she was going to like these two. Leeba went on to say that she and Anat would alternate visits. Leeba would talk about language and speech therapy and Anat would concentrate on learning the ways in which Cate could meet her own needs, to use language and behavior to her advantage.

Neely sat quietly listening to their story as it was told to Cate and Jenny.

Leeba and Anat were a formidable team. They had met in graduate school where they studied psychology at the University of Chicago. Upon completion of their graduate studies, they continued their friendship in a journey to Israel to devote a year to in-depth understanding of their heritage. "We went to be a part of a kibbutz. That word in Hebrew means 'group.'"

"We found immense gratification in planting trees, draining swamps, and other hard-graft efforts to make a formidable land farmable and livable," Leeba explained. "These were powerful pulls for us to learn more about our past history. After that year in Israel, we returned to America to work with Dr. Brickman." With what they believed to be another dimension of understanding that would enhance their training, they were ready to do their work.

Neely thought, "I must remember to ask Leeba and Anat how they had come to work for Dr. Brickman and how the three of them had made their way to the valley." Their Jewish background intrigued Neely, and she was already planning ways to bring more of their culture and others to Kilhaven, especially to Cate and Sean. Neely loved the mixture of Judaism, Presbyterianism, Scots-Irish, and the little red-head Catholic. Christmas would be a perfect time for such.

But now it was back to reality. They had met Cate. They had seen her in action and all the seminars, conferences, classrooms, internships, degrees, and trips to Israel could not truly prepare them for the first full-blown episode of anxiety and anger that they witnessed in their tiny client. This was their first professional experience with an autistic child, and Cate was not totally innocent. She was clever, she was loud, and she knew what buttons to push to get a desired reaction.

The two young women wondered at times how such a pretty little thing could make so much noise and show so much temper. Her outbursts were on display often in the beginning; perhaps because Jenny had her own chores to do and sought to use this time when Cate was with this new team to get those chores done. This angered Cate, and she chose various means to express it.

Her favorite trick was to put her hands in Leeba's hair and pull it forward, frequently pulling it so hard that it was painful.

Anat wondered if Cate loved the idea that Leeba was sitting in the darkness of her own hair, unable to see out, vulnerable and under Cate's power. At other times she would crawl over Anat, putting her feet in Anat's lap. The debate that ensued between these young therapists was over how to react. Leeba was inclined to stay calm, low-key, exhibit little if any reaction.

Anat felt otherwise. "She is disrespecting you, Leeba. She puts you in a position where she has control over you and whether or not you can see."

"No, you are wrong," Leeba responded. "She is playing. She would not be aware of respect or recognize such a social cue."

This debate continued over time and each of them moved to the middle and just tried to adapt to the situations as they arose. The plan had been for them to come separately, but in the beginning they found comfort and support by going together. They were no longer in the kibbutz; they were on the front lines of reality.

Neely came to believe that the major difficulty of dealing with an autistic person lies in the inability to get inside the mind of the autistic person. She knew the possibility of taking images of the autistic brain, therefore looking into the brain. She knew of the ability to compare those images to a normal brain of a person who is not autistic. But this picture is not for translation into an understanding of motivation or thought processes. Understanding comes from time and experience and trust and those professionals who seek to find the real answers. Time she had, trust she had found, and experience she was gaining.

Chapter Fourteen

The early snow did come, but it didn't last, and the unusually frigid temperatures made Jenny grateful that Pearl and Simus had cleared the last of the garden. They had canned and filled every Mason jar they had and bought a case or two more. The jams and jellies would see them through the winter and the vegetables would keep them from eating food that someone else had prepared. They had eventually bought a pig for bacon, but no one could bring themselves to kill it so it just became another Kilhaven pet that they named Shortie.

One day that fall, Neely was back in the parlor in deep thought. She had something on her mind that was a worry. She was pleased with the things that were being accomplished with Cate, who had only recently decided to trust Leeba and Anat. Although they really did seem to know how to engage her, more importantly they cared.

They had been coming to Kilhaven for a few months now and had come to be very comfortable with Cate. She had slowly warmed to them and, on a day when they had planned to paint in the barn, she seemed overly enthusiastic and anxious to show them her work. They wisely avoided asking about the images and in a gesture that seemed much like appreciation and approval, Cate began to shout. "Alice, Alice!"

"Alice, what?" Leeba said.

And in a string of words that made their point, Cate said, "I'm not Alice, I'm Alice. Please thank you, call me Alice." That signal of acceptance and trust was the basis of a new relationship between the three of them.

The reports back from Anat and Leeba to Neely were both positive and candid, the latter not always being easy to take. Neely felt guilty that so much effort and money was being spent on Cate and that Sean was often left to his own devices. He too had his own quirks; he was also a finicky eater but, all in all, he was an outstanding boy. He cared for his sister but had begun to verbally express his frustration that everything had to shift in her favor. No one wanted to stir up her temper; the results were just too unpleasant. A pattern of peacekeeping developed and it mainly served Cate, causing Sean justifiable resentment.

To everyone's great surprise, perhaps in part to feel he was in control of something, Sean decided he wanted to be called Michael. All concerned were having great difficulty in making the change. It was his own personal selection of a name. Jenny balked at first, claiming "I can't all of a sudden switch and call that boy Michael," but of course, she did.

He treasured the time spent with his Grandfather O'Malley, which may have been why he chose to go by the same name. He loved to hear stories of his father and Ireland and fishing. Though Grandfather was aging, he was mindful of this boy's need for a man in his life and made sure that he was always available to Michael. He let him ride with him on the new tractor, a therapeutic act in light of what had happened to his father. Michael was nine now and old enough for what Grandfather O'Malley considered to be life lessons. He told Michael, "When you fall off a horse, you have to get up and get back on." He knew what had happened to his father and could see what his Grandfather wanted him to know.

He taught Michael to play dominos, bait a hook, bat a ball, fly a kite, and row a boat. He could not help him with his new math, for he had never known it, but he could teach him how to mow the field, plant a crop, and raise some calves. But the most important thing that Grandfather O'Malley did for his grandson was to be a model of integrity, honesty, manners, kindness, and respect for others. He loved Cate, but at times felt at a loss in knowing exactly what to say or do. So he sat with her and watched movies. When she could sit still, he would read to her.

Neely also loved to spend time with Michael. He looked so much like his father. He was interested in music and reading and they went to movies together. Even though he was young, when he asked to have a small violin, she took him to the city to purchase one and then found him a teacher. He seemed to have a natural talent for the instrument and Neely would take him to his special lessons twice a week.

At the same time and after much discussion, Neely decided to have Cate homeschooled. Things had not gone well that year without Laura to smooth things over. Cate needed a school that had a special education component but also had teacher assistants. Cate did not want to go and Neely's doubts and fears when she had heard that Laura's contract had not been renewed had been well founded.

Cate had been agitated from the very first bell. The shrill sound of the intercom hurt her ears, the other students taunted her, the teachers did not seem to want her in the classroom, a number of parents objected to her presence, and the smell of the food served there made her sick to her stomach. She was expected to eat combinations of food, even when she could plainly see there were "bugs."

Her outbursts were unnerving to all around her. But it was unnerving to Cate as well and the layering of her frustration culminated in two dramatic events. In the first, she choked another student, and in the second, she punched her teacher in the stomach. Neely was forced to bring Cate home. That was fine with Cate. She didn't want to go in the first place.

Chapter Fifteen

For the first time it entered Neely's head that Sean, now Michael, needed more; more of his own space and a world separate from his sister who was usually making trouble for him. His resentment had become a reality. He relished the fact that his father had been a Millford student and he had expressed an interest in going there. Though it was a preparatory school, it had a middle school that would have met his needs. At nine, as he entered fourth grade, he was ready to go.

As Neely drove up the long drive to Millford, she could see that it was a lovely place. It looked proud of itself with its red brick, its tall columns and carefully planted pansies in large clay pots. "They must have a gardener," she thought. "No wonder it is so expensive." The windows were glistening and the paint on the tall wooden doors looked prim in their newly acquired coats of white. The brass plaque to the right of the door clearly indicated that this was an important building, one recognized for its longevity, having been established in 1910. It was officially and historically old! It was feeling more and more like this was the place for Michael.

Neely was pleasantly surprised when a cheerful young woman met her and ushered her into the waiting room of Millford's headmaster. She looked up to see a distinguished young man with neatly trimmed blonde hair and wearing a comfortable sweater under his jacket. Striding leisurely toward her, he extended his hand for a welcoming handshake. Any intimidation she had felt was put quickly at ease in his office when she was seated across from Avery Millford, a great-grandson of the original headmaster.

Mr. Millford was a good listener and Neely found herself telling her story with all its joys and sorrows. Later she reproached herself for being so forthcoming with a perfect stranger, but it had seemed so natural at the time and she could use a good therapist, even in the person of a headmaster.

Her decision to send Michael to Millford School was a very good decision. He was ready for something new and as things became more difficult with Cate, all agreed that this might be for the best. Neely also felt he deserved as much as she could give him. And Michael entered Millford.

Grandfather O'Malley drove Michael the twenty miles to and from school each day, and it became a special time when he could talk to his grandson about the day's experiences. It reminded him of the days when he drove his own son to Millford and it helped to mend some of the wounds of his loss. Neely felt that Michael was in good hands both with his grandfather and with Millford's headmaster, Mr. Avery Millford.

Cate remained happily at home. She busied herself with her therapies, drawing, painting, and movies. On one afternoon shortly after Leeba and Anat had left Kilhaven, Jenny found Cate bundled up but painting her art pictures on the screened porch.

"Cate, it is way too cold for you to be out here; you come on back in this house." Cate ignored the statement and continued her painting. Jenny repeated herself to the same reaction. She was perturbed and as she started to gather up the art work Cate started screaming, "I'm late, I'm late."

Jenny said, "Late for what?" No answer.

With a sigh, Cate picked up her work, which was a dramatic drawing of what appeared to be figures at some common event. They were brightly colored in happy yellows, pinks, and purples. She walked into the kitchen, seemingly upset, she turned and scowling at Jenny screamed, "A party…the Hatter's party…I'm Alice. I'm Alice and I'm late." In that moment, Cate was in both her worlds—the one with Jenny in the kitchen and the other at a tea party with the sleepy Dormouse listening to stories and riddles.

It took a minute for Jenny to realize what this meant. She was shocked to learn that, after all these years, Cate's favorite name, "Alice," had been chosen because she was a little girl at a tea party with the March Hare in Wonderland. She left clues for the family to hear as she was prone to quote "mad as a March Hare." But they did not hear. Now she would finally say, "I am not Alice, (just plain Alice that is)." Clearly, she was Alice in Wonderland.

Chapter Sixteen

B ut not all those in Wonderland were as happy as they might have been. In fact, things looked more like the confusion in Lewis Carroll's rabbit hole. The vestiges of the March Hare and the Mad Hatter were in evidence. All things associated with Wonderland had left a mark and it lasted for a very long time.

By age nine, Cate had developed an expanded vocabulary; the only problem was that she would not use it. Was it because it was easier not to do so? Or in her mind was it sufficient to her need? Whatever her reason for still hoping to get by with using one word at a time, Neely spent much time encouraging her to put words together in a meaningful way. Still Cate had her own ideas. Her favorite word was "again." She used it to indicate a desire to repeat an experience.

Cate: "Again."

Neely: "Again what?"

Cate: "Again, please."

Neely: "Again, please, what?"

Cate: "Again, please PLAY BALL"

Cate received a gummy bear!

Cate could be rambunctious. Still at the age of nine, if she didn't get her way, she had more and more severe outbursts. Her bad behavior seemed to escalate to new levels. She had more of everything. She had more words, more stimulation, more experiences, and it is likely that she was more often jarred from her inner world.

Content in her own world, she did not want to be interrupted, and if that happened, there was a price to be paid by the "interrupter." Cate would then launch into a loud and unpleasant stream of senseless words strung together with no apparent connection. It could be described as if, for her, there was a non-stop internal monologue. If that internal monologue was interrupted by an external monologue, such as a comment from another person, Cate became extremely agitated, going into a rage of seemingly irrelevant thoughts or claims.

"I'm home, Cate. What are you doing?" Neely said coming through the back door.

Cate immediately started her shouting. "What…what!"… humming…"Repeat…repeat."…pause…"Again…again." The eyes blinked, the hands flailed. "That and that."…nodding, then the discordant repetition would begin again, "I'm bad."… pause…"I'm, bad."

Blinking eyes were just one of the many quirks that Cate manifested. Neely tried to explain it to Jenny and Pearl.

"The 'quirks' are called 'stims' and are a form of 'self-calming.'" Neely was always reluctant to know how to handle these stims. Some she observed in Cate were the repeated protrusion of her tongue, often causing sores around her mouth, or sticking her tongue inside her chin, or walking hunched over for days, humming, walking backwards while kicking herself on her bottom with the foot not on the ground, or lying down on her stomach on a flat surface. Most stims did not last for more than a month and then a new habit would surface. These stims were a regular aspect of Cate's behavior. She may or may not have been aware, but in any case she did not seem to care and they were often exposed at inappropriate times.

Cate had always been afraid of water, even as a baby. Later when she had words, she would say, "Sharks in there. Sharks in ocean," which she had seen in movies. Bathing was traumatic. She also refused to have her hair or nails trimmed without a major confrontation. "Hurts…hurts," she would scream. Even

Jenny could not convince her that nails and hair do not hurt. She would claim, "I'm bad." She did not really mean that she thought she was bad, rather it was just something to say, likely a line from a movie or cartoon. But even in the face of such convoluted behaviors and thoughts, Neely was patient and kind and could connect with Cate.

Neely would say to herself, "I must stay calm. If I become upset or show any sign of concern, Cate becomes even more upset. I know what upsets her. She loves to be touched and I love to hold her. Spending time with her is fascinating. I find her as charming and interesting as anyone I have ever known."

In reflecting on her special relationship with this little girl, Neely realized that there was a compassion and sensitivity in Cate that brought an added dimension of understanding from her, as she was always aware of the emotional state of her mother. This was in direct contrast to what she had read regarding lack of sensitivity and social cues of others. But Neely would cling to those moments of sympathy and concern as they seemed to bring to the surface, that mysterious part of Cate, somehow joining the two of them in a special way.

Cate knew the difference between an allergy sniffle and a tearful emotional upset. She would say, "Mommy crying? Don't cry, Mommy. Here's a tissue, you're OK," she would repeat with utmost concern. Despite her many outbursts and disconnects, she was also incredibly loving and caring and, when she wanted to, she could make a sentence.

Neely would say with considerable gratitude, "She seems to want to be with me."

Once when Neely had a meeting at Saint Patrick's, Cate asked, "Can I go Mommy?"

Neely explained, "No, it's boring for kids."

Cate responded, "No, it's good! It's good for kids!" Neely could not resist that.

In spite of the fact that "autism" means something like "alone," Cate would do almost anything to avoid sleeping by herself. Often in the wee hours of the morning, she would sneak into bed with Neely or her grandmother. Jack the dog was a favorite and the cats would give her a wide berth!

It helped those at Kilhaven to put away the unpleasant aspects of the disorder and focus on the endearing moments that encouraged those who were there to care, no matter the difficulty. It was important to remember the good times and what made Cate so special. Neely could hear Cate's desire to please when she really wanted something and would string together every polite word she could think of.

Neely would say, "Do you want to go to the library?"

Cate's response would be "No thank you, please, I'm good."

Neely was amazed at Cate's art. The drawings were so fascinating; the animals or people had perfectly expressive faces and their tiny feet seemed poised for any and all sorts of action. There were also the creative inventions such as creatures made from play dough. She loved to pose them for pictures.

Neely would say, "Living with Cate is a magical experience. It is about finding little gems of creativity and fascination when least expected."

She showed an astounded Grace O'Malley a favorite letter that Cate had typed on Neely's computer. It read:

Dear Frog, Beaverboy and Raccoon,

We know you're magic. Free Birds is the door right there. It's over there near the handles and craft boards. Free Birds is over near there. It's right there. A Big small door, it's near the Stonefield, the right door. Not the left door. It's right there. Beaverboy, Raccoon, Frog, Jack and I had to leave back to the brown house. I will go back to the tree. And now, come to my house.

Love,
Alice O'Malley

To Neely it was magical.

Reactions to Cate were different among the household. For Jenny, Cate was her baby. With no child of her own, she gave her all. She loved Cate, it was that simple. Pearl occasionally slipped out during one of the unpleasant outbursts but she too gave all the love she had to give. The O'Malleys were dismayed and disheartened at times. This was a situation beyond their understanding yet they never stopped trying. They transferred all their feelings for their lost son to Cate and Michael, providing them with all their resources. It would always be so, even after they were gone. Thankfully, with Sean Michael's insurance, Grace and Michael's inheritance and invested savings, their estate was sufficient to provide for their needs for the rest of their lives and for Cate that would always be crucial.

Chapter Seventeen

In addition to autism, Cate had been diagnosed with "intellectual disability." Neely learned these were two distinctly separate diagnoses. At one time, the latter was referred to as "mental retardation." The prognosis was that she would likely stall in her emotional development around the age of four and that was precisely what happened. Her social skills were erratic and her motivation puzzling. A second try at school was attempted when Miss Laura was rehired for Cate's third grade year. Even though Cate was troublesome, especially when in school, she had always had a certain few classmates that were drawn to her. "Come sit by me," one would say, and she might or might not accommodate. At the same time, she could never meet the educational goals.

Her interests were in objects, not people. She had great dexterity and balance. By age ten, she could type and punctuate to perfection. By age eleven, she could memorize easily and, with her obsession with movies, she would often borrow from the dialogue.

She assigned the names of famous stars to the people she knew. Her favorites included Harrison Ford which she assigned to Simus, Angelina Jolie which was given to Neely, and Neil Patrick Harris which she gave to Michael. Lesser known featured characters were used to express that internal monologue. Cate was in one's presence, but she was not with you.

It was not unusual for her to walk up to an oriental person and say: "You're Bruce Lee!" She would also identify any African American woman as, "You're Whoopie Goldberg!"

She would walk up to a stranger and say, "What's your name?" Most people would realize that this was a special child and politely respond with something like "My name is Bill, what's yours?" Some would shrug their shoulders and scratch their heads. Some would be embarrassed and stare. Some would react with sympathy. There were those who understood.

Although there were many special people in Cate's life, only a few really truly knew how to connect with her. In the first grade it had been Miss Laura who understood the problems she faced and knew how to handle them. She was devoted to Cate and was with her, assisting her in the many tasks that must have seemed impossible.

However, the school had not seen how important Laura was to Cate and had not renewed her contract for the second grade. Cate had been devastated. Miss Laura had been greatly missed and in her absence the school finally came to recognize her ability to connect with Cate. At Neely's request, they rehired her for the last time for the third grade. Cate's third grade began successful, but it did not last. That was her last year in school. It was back to homeschooling.

Certainly it is rare to find a person who understands autistic problems and has the knowledge to deal with the difficulties that are inevitable. It was after the third grade that the real trouble came and the result was that Cate had to be schooled at home. The school simply did not cover her needs. She didn't care. She would go home again.

Neely concluded to herself, "Some segments of society try to relegate the autistic and otherwise 'differently disabled' to metaphorical social graves. But they can still rebound and remind us of their vibrancy and rightful claim to life in all its many aspects."

Neely remembered Monty Python was known to say, "Bring out your dead!" Then the unwillingly transported "ill" quipped, "I'm not dead yet." She did not want Cate to be counted out.

Chapter Eighteen

A year went by. Jenny, Pearl, and Simus did their part to keep things going. Grandfather O'Malley had brought more cattle onto the land the year before and now had a pasture solely for what he called "the cowgirls." It was the maternity field and in the spring when the babies were born, it was pure joy for ten-year-old Cate to watch the little ones scamper after their mamas hoping for a meal. Grandfather took great pleasure in letting Cate bottle feed the baby calves.

Grandfather just needed something to do, an increased demand on his time. Michael was at Millford, and time hung heavy. Having retired the year before at sixty-five, he still had plenty of energy and enthusiasm left in him and therefore he extended his holdings. This action required a larger barn, a project he turned over to Simus. To build it, Simus brought in all his cousins.

Some of those cousins came from as far away as West Virginia, some from just across Sand Creek Holler. The Drummond boys, Carey, Duff, and Fergus, were all sons of Eubie Drummond, Jenny's first cousin. They were good people and hard workers and they were family. They had been brought up to believe that hard work was the answer to all of life's problems and that it brought its own rewards.

On the final day of the barn raising, Jenny and Pearl turned the whole thing into what they called a "shindig." To them, celebrating always included some dancing and playing their banjos. They had fried catfish, hush puppies, grits, green beans, cornbread muffins, tomatoes, onions, watermelon, and apple pie. It was a jubilant celebration with laughter, music, singing, and shouting for joy. Everyone there stood back more than once to admire their new red barn.

These were good folks but the barn raisers, with a little help from their imbibing, turned into hell raisers. A keg of beer provided temptation and inspiration. So it was that all the Drummond boys "dreamin' up some entertainment," decided to have some fun. They danced with each other until they couldn't move and they chased a rabbit but it got away. Fergus played his banjo and everyone joined in to sing all their favorites. They had great fun, but the laughter and cheering that ensued was more than Cate could tolerate.

No one had noticed how Cate's behavior had changed. The noise so agitated and disturbed her that she began to scream, "No! No!"

Neely consoled her, "It's OK, Cate."

"No, I'm bad," she said. Cate threw herself on the ground and screamed and rolled. She finally ran behind the barn and, before anyone realized it, she had disappeared.

For the next several hours, everyone looked for Cate. The celebration was brought to an abrupt halt—a premature and disappointing ending. Soon the barn builders became a search party. The sun was setting and clouds were rolling in. The clash of thunder alerted the searchers that a storm and darkness would probably soon be upon them. Indeed, Mother Nature chose that time to send heavy rains. Unprepared and with not so much as an umbrella, the searchers were forced to face the wet and darkness head on.

Given Cate's great fear of water, the searchers could only hope that she would stay away from the pond and the creek, but that was a real danger and they went there looking for her more than once. There were times when she could be vindictive, even punitive and would seem to reach into herself to retaliate against those who had offended her. She had been offended by all the noise and she would punish those who had caused it. She was simply angry and frightened.

Neely, Grace, Grandfather O'Malley, Michael, Simus and the Drummond boys scoured every inch of Kilhaven. Everyone was frantic; most of all the O'Malleys who feared another tragedy. Neely and Simus checked and rechecked the pond. Jenny and Pearl went through the meadow. Their fears became greater as the hours passed. Darkness was upon them. They called her name repeatedly but there was no answer.

Around midnight, Jenny went back to the house to make coffee for the search party. As she approached the back door she noticed a dim light through a small attic window. She sprang up those stairs as fast as her legs would carry her, hurriedly opened the door and found Cate flat on her stomach where she had fallen asleep after surrounding herself with bold paintings in streaks of red and black. One suggested figures of people with tiny bodies and great huge heads. One had the semblance of a structure colored red like the barn. IT WAS ON FIRE. These were paintings that, for once, there was no need to guess at their meanings. THIS was Cate's reality.

How could one be angry at a child for being frightened? Afterward, Neely held Cate tightly and read to her from one of her favorite books, *The Runaway Bunny* by Margaret Wise Brown, a charming story about a bunny who thinks he will run away but whose mother always finds him. It seemed appropriate for this day.

Chapter Nineteen

Christmas of 1993 was approaching and the house was about to put on its fancy dress. At Kilhaven this was a bit different from most homes. Over the years, this house in the Shenandoah Valley had morphed into a cultural mix that served the needs of all who found a place therein. Of course there was that O'Malley Irish thing, the Catholic aspect, and now that Leeba and Anat had become a part of the family, there was the Jewish thing. They all got together and decided that to complete their seasonal celebration they would add the traditional Kwanzaa celebration.

Neely and Grace O'Malley wanted to bring as much of the outside world to their home and children as possible. They embraced the differences in cultures as a reflection of affirming Cate's differences. All together this purported some lengthy and lavish celebration of the season. Neely was in charge of keeping track of the various activities, especially all the lightings of the various meaningful candles.

So, in early December, everyone involved at Kilhaven began to observe Hanukkah. Each night for eight days they lit the special menorah with its eight candles lit one at a time each evening at sundown. Cate took a special delight in the candle lighting and wanted everyone to sing each evening. They would burn the candle for a half hour and according to some, exchange a small gift with each lighting. Leeba and Anat liked to say "It is not to light within, but to illuminate the home without." It was honoring their spiritual life and blessings.

Cate especially liked the part about opening a gift each night and asked repeatedly for *The Little Mermaid*, a movie, which of course she received. This Hans Christian Andersen tale became her new favorite and she watched it over and over, learning and using its sounds, words and rhythms.

It was during Hanukkah that everyone gathered, piled in the back of the old rusty Chevy pickup truck, and with eyes wide open, shared the joy of looking for the perfect Christmas tree. It had to be tall, it had to be full, and it had to be beautiful. There was little disagreement in their choice once the tallest, fullest, most beautiful tree was found. Once it was loaded, the would-be decorators dutifully walked behind, laughing, singing and declaring as they had in the previous year, that it was indeed "the most beautiful tree ever."

Simus mounted the tree in its stand and with a little help from Grandfather O'Malley, carried it in to the parlor and placed it in the corner next to the windows. Outside, winter was in all its glory with the oaks and elms in a stark state of undress in their long seasonal nap. Those trees would later consider a spring wardrobe but for now they were on the outside looking in and watching Christmas happen. The trees were handsomely decorated with strings of popcorn and cranberries.

Simus carefully laid a fire in the fireplace and kept it going throughout each day. Neely spent time in the parlor and had carefully placed the greens on the mantel and the candles in the window.

Most outsiders would have considered that Christmas at Kilhaven a bit overdone, but it was a time when these weary folks could pause and actually enjoy a child's level of living. The family worked hard to decorate the house with traditional holly and berries. The glow in each window was a standing invitation to all who came near. Bright colors reached out from every corner.

The family carefully lit the tree and decorated it with ornaments that were greeted like precious old friends. These ornaments had been with the family long enough to have personalities; each had a special memory of origin that brought sentiment and laughter from those who carefully took them from their boxes. It was a happy time for Cate as she painted pictures in reds and greens or purple and pink, whatever struck her fancy, then cut them into smaller ornaments to hang on the tree. Grandmother Grace carefully made little thread hangers for each colorful ornament. This was a tree affectionately embraced by a child's abstractions; only Cate knew what they represented but to her they were beautiful. She squealed with delight with each individual addition.

As the family gathered around the fire in the evening, Cate and Michael at his feet, Grandfather O'Malley would talk about the Irish Christmas traditions that he had learned from his parents. He had heard about the lively horse races on Saint Stephen's Day, which for some was simply a good excuse to drink with friends. There were also the Christmas day swims that took place all over Ireland when hundreds of people jumped off a rock into the Irish Sea wearing only their bathing suits.

Grandfather O'Malley continued, "Oddly, another Irish tradition is the reading of 'The Dead,' a transcendent tale by James Joyce, and a reflection on our past, our present and future, which has rather become like an Irish version of Charles Dickens's *A Christmas Carol*." Also, there was "the awful Christmas sweater," which was almost like a competition in the streets of Ireland, the more tacky and ridiculous the better. Grandfather was delighted to recall a sweater of his own father that had once won a prize. He laughed as he said, "It was truly ugly!"

Traditionally, in this Irish Catholic home, decorations would go up on December 8, the Feast of the Immaculate Conception, and come down on January 6, the Feast of the Epiphany. And while the Conception and the Epiphany were most important, those "feasts" were of equal measure. In between those dates there would be caroling, cooking, eating, drinking, and above all, Midnight Mass on Christmas Eve with all the liturgy, pageantry, choirs, and affirmation that comes from the collective mind and spirit. Michael and Cate were much the center of attention and spent hours with Grandmother and Grandfather O'Malley or in the kitchen baking with Jenny.

Yet another glorious aspect of this unusual house at Christmas was the celebration of Kwanzaa honoring the African heritage. Kwanzaa was a week-long recognition that included iconic images of soul food and at this time of the year almonds oranges, and raisins. The groaning board for Christmas Eve supper consisted of oyster stew, country ham, yeast bread, blackberry jelly, cakes, and cookies.

In addition to the holly and pine cones, the house was decorated with Kwanzaa's objects of art and colorful cloth. A decoration mat was carefully placed to display the Kinara holding the seven candles with their seven principles and celebrating African history and religion. Cate's brightly colored art was perfect for Kwanzaa. She even made small name tags for everyone. Grace, with her gift for languages greeted everyone each day with "Hab ari Gani?" Swahili for "what's the news?" Michael proudly provided the drums and music. It was also a chance for him to play his violin. The entire family celebrated each and every rich aspect of this cultural and spiritual season at Kilhaven.

On Christmas Eve after Mass, Cate and Michael hung their stockings from the mantel. Theirs were not the fancy velvet kind with sequins; theirs were the huge woolen ones that belonged to their grandfather and had been knitted by their grandmother. Grace had carefully made them as a gift to her husband, but they had soon become a part of their Christmas tradition. Christmas morning they had been mysteriously filled by Santa who favored fruit and nuts.

And so it was that at Kilhaven in December you could hear the heartfelt greetings of "Happy Hanukkah!" or "Joyous Kwanzaa!" or "Merry Christmas!" It was a celebration of difference that was actually all about the same thing.

Chapter Twenty

Afew years had passed since Michael had been enrolled at Millford. He was very happy there. He had achieved a place on the Honor Roll, taken a chair in the violin section of the school orchestra, excelled at sports, and was very popular. He was proud to be in the same school that his father had attended. Neely felt that she had done the right thing in sending him there. And to support this, she had joined the Millford Parents' Association.

Still, it was a great surprise when the phone rang at home one afternoon and Neely heard, "Mrs. O'Malley? This is Avery Millford."

Neely's heart turned over as she considered all the possibilities for this call and none of them were good. Michael had not mentioned being in trouble but certainly this could happen without her knowing about it. "Yes, Mr. Millford, how nice of you to call."

He continued, "Well, just to put your mind at ease, I am not calling about Michael, he is a very good student and a really nice young man. You should be very proud."

"Yes, I am proud." Neely replied, then wondered to herself, "So why is he calling?"

"Well actually, this is a social call. I was wondering if I might take you out to dinner?"

Neely felt weak in the knees. This was the last thing she had expected and she hardly knew what to say. She had been a widow for more than ten years now and the only men in her life were Grandfather, Michael III, and Simus. To say the least, she was taken aback. "Well, Mr. Millford I don't know; well, I suppose I would be able to have dinner with you."

He responded enthusiastically. "Wonderful, I was thinking of Friday evening; I know a place down by the river and I hear it's nice. What about 7:00?"

Neely replied, "That sounds nice. Thank you."

And so the scene was set for an evening out with Mr. Millford.

Neely thought to herself, "Oh God, do I want to do this? Do I even know how to do this?" Going out for dinner with a man was now so far removed from her thinking that she felt a shiver run through her body. She knew it was only dinner but she had to wonder if she should even consider such a dimension to her life that was already so full of responsibilities. She wondered what the children would think and what the O'Malleys would think.

As she walked in to the kitchen she looked at Grace and Jenny. She knew they must have overheard her conversation and she began to defend herself. "Well, I was caught off guard. I really should call him back and say I can't go."

Both Grace and Jenny immediately sprang into action with encouragement. "Of course you are going," Grace said and Jenny agreed.

So Friday came and Neely met Mr. Millford at the door. Her heart was beating very fast and it was mostly because this was an unusual situation and she wasn't sure how she felt about it. But as he stepped in the door she felt the same comfort she had experienced that first day at Millford. He was nicely dressed as if this was really important. She was impressed.

The little restaurant on the river was nice. The atmosphere was friendly and conducive to their getting acquainted. As they talked, the color of the river changed from a clear warm green with a cast from the late-day sun, to a deep rich olive embellished by the darkness. As evening turned to night, a thin sliver of a moon, blocked by planet Earth, made its way through the steady flow of the water. They talked and talked with ease and discovered an instant friendship peppered with subtle possibilities.

Avery Millford was the fourth generation in his family to embrace the business of educating young boys to become outstanding men. Their academic standards were impressive and consistent. All the Millfords had been completely dedicated to the school and to the young people who passed through their halls.

"May I call you Neely?" he had asked.

Caught off guard, she said, "Oh, of course."

"And you will call me Avery?" he asked.

Neely responded, "Well, that would be just fine." It was thus settled, they were now on first-name basis.

Realizing the moon had made a dramatic move to the west, they left the restaurant. He drove her home, pressed her hand, and said goodnight. The earth continued to spin on its axis.

Chapter Twenty-One

With that semi-formal genesis, a new relationship began. The two were well suited. They were both attractive, bright, educated, shared interests in literature, and were curious about the world, and they were both widowed.

Neely was very beautiful and had learned to be tough under a porcelain veneer. She had been part of a respectable family. Her father was a grim, foreboding, difficult man with a bad temper. Her mother was compliant and submissive, with a tendency toward hypochondria, but always was one to accommodate her husband's demands.

Neely's mother and her sister, Neely's aunt and Cate's namesake, had been estranged, mainly because her sister had defended Neely's choice to marry a Catholic. This endeared her to Neely and since she essentially had no member of her family to stand with her, it was Aunt Mary Caitlin who she had asked to be the godmother of her baby girl. The child would have been christened at Saint Patrick's but for her unpredictable infant behavior. She and Michael were ultimately christened at Kilhaven by Father Fleming. The godmother was unable to attend. No one ever knew why. The Burkes declined an invitation to attend and that became Neely's last attempt at a reconciliation with them.

Had she been asked, Neely would likely say that her childhood was not unpleasant. All her physical needs had been met, but she would also say that it was not really pleasant. She was an only child and lonely much of the time as her parents went about their way, doing what they deemed essential and never seeming to have the time to stop and love their one daughter.

Work, social involvement, and a considerable commitment to their church took much of their day. There was little time for Neely, and she sensed that there was more to life than she had witnessed in her parents. It was a thrill when she went away to college and met young Sean Michael O'Malley.

Their romance was a true matter of the heart. There was an instant chemistry and, as they grew in their relationship, they knew very soon that they would ultimately marry. Neely must have had at least a hunch that her parents would disapprove, recalling their reaction when she had gone home one weekend just to tell them she was dating Sean Michael. They had strongly disapproved, and she remembered breaking out in a rash from her nervousness. She had continued to see him anyway. .

When speaking with them concerning marriage, she was not asking permission. She was making a declaration, Neely would not let Sean Michael ask. The outcome was heartbreaking. She had never considered the possibility that she might have to choose between Sean Michael and her own parents. When it became clear that this was her option, Neely was shattered. Forced to choose, Sean Michael was her choice. Later, when tragedy took him, the depth of pain had been very great and beyond her imagination. During the past decade she had made her children her new choice. There was no alternative.

Avery Millford had also lost his choice. A widower for the past four years, he had immersed himself in his work and had sorely neglected any effort at a social life. He had been impressed with Neely when she first came to Millford to seek admission for Michael. Even though Neely had admonished herself at the time for divulging so much of herself, Avery had listened and he liked what he heard. He especially admired her devotion to Cate, along with her acceptance and desire to create a place of comfort for her. He witnessed her love and pride in both her children.

Avery had been happy in a marriage that had ended in sadness because of the extended illness that had taken his wife of seven years. They had no children. Soon after his wife died, meeting Neely was the first glimmer of thought concerning any kind of new experience. However, few more years went by before he felt ready to take the next step.

Their similar loss was perhaps the initial basis of their connection beyond the professional definition linked to Millford. After their dinner down by the river, that connection was intensified with the feelings each experienced, which were mixed excitement and apprehension. Neely felt especially apprehensive. She realized the confounding aspects of her life that came with her as a package, and even at that early stage of friendship, she acknowledged the possibilities and complications that she brought to any situation. Yet she was reluctant to back away. It had been so long and so difficult and she felt happy with Avery.

Friendship became romance and Neely realized that there was a challenge that had to be faced. Avery and Cate had to meet. Avery loved Neely and she loved him. She welcomed the warmth and support that he brought to her life. Everyone at Kilhaven really liked Avery. Clearly the O'Malleys approved, and that lifted a great concern from Neely. With their encouragement, accompanied by Neely's fear and trepidation, plans were made for a meeting between Cate and Avery.

It was a Sunday, with Avery invited to a meal in the dining room. Kilhaven seemed to sense that this day was special, and it was as if all the oaks and elms were smiling in approval. Avery was gracious and pleasant. He arrived bearing a lovely bouquet of flowers for Grace and some dark chocolate for Grandfather O'Malley. He brought some new markers for Cate. He brought a violin recording for Michael. For Neely, there was a tiny Millford pin to be worn on her lapel.

He won the household over at the front door and it was not because of his gifts; they really liked him. They joked that he had brought so many things but they loved the thoughts and he seemed pleased. He relaxed a bit when he saw young Michael and the comfortable feelings were reciprocated.

Jenny was in the kitchen humming and preparing some of her personal favorites. Pearl was giddy with excitement. She announced, "Jenny, I'll take the chicken in. I want to see Mr. Millford." With the greatest ceremony they presented the day's menu, and it was received with the greatest of gratitude.

Avery wondered why Cate did not eat with them but was too polite to ask. Conversation came easily over dinner. They talked of the farm, the cows in the pasture, new requirements at Millford, Avery's father, and plans for the school.

As the last dish was cleared, Neely invited Avery to the parlor to meet Cate. They settled in the chairs by the fireplace. Avery had the markers handy and ready for presentation. At first, Cate refused to come out of the kitchen. Even Jenny's urging was met with an obstinance unlike any she had ever exhibited. Only when Neely coaxed her with an invitation to show her art, did she relent.

Upon being introduced to Avery, she froze. She stared at him for a long time, then she stared at her mother and started to scream, she ran toward Avery beating his chest, scratching his face, kicking him then putting her hands around his neck as if to choke him. She turned to a nearby table overturning a vase, which she then picked up and threw against the wall. She tore her art into tiny pieces and finally turning back to his face she screamed, "I AM ALICE! I AM ALICE, YOU ARE NOT THE WHITE RABBIT. NO, NO! THIS IS NOT A TEA PARTY! DON'T CALL ME ALICE!" And, glaring at Avery, she yelled, "WE'LL ALL BE KILLED!"

Chapter Twenty-Two

The house was silent. Neely was alone in the parlor. Avery had left. The thoughts in her head just would not unscramble. Jenny had taken Cate upstairs and the rest of the family had dispersed, each with their own thoughts and dismay. Neely replayed this day and its events over and over in her head and as she put her head in her hands, she sobbed with a lifetime of tears.

The next time she saw Avery was on the following Saturday. It was as if each of them had needed some time to let events settle. Avery had been on the phone to reassure Neely that somehow, someway they would manage to work through this together. He assured her that he was still there in all the same ways and that it would be just fine. Neely wanted to believe that.

Their relationship, which existed separately from the rest of Neely's life, was good and right but any hint of what remained from that Sunday with Avery and Cate cast a darkness over what was the balance of her life. Avery continued to attempt a friendship with Cate, but the harsh reality was delivered with each outburst that took place on every encounter.

Avery had tried to approach Cate through her art, asking to see some of her work. She balked. He brought her a new movie, something about a little girl from France, but she refused to accept it, in fact she threw it at him. He asked her to show him around the barn to see the new calves, but she was not interested. He suggested a long drive with her mother along, but she declined.

So it was that all Avery's efforts failed in spite of his warrior-worthy determination. He could perhaps have outlasted Cate but all concerned were weary.

Neely thought her hair was turning gray. The apprehension in her heart grew each day. Once again she found herself full of questions. What should she expect? What did she deserve? The totality of loss had been unbearable. There was Sean Michael, her parents, and Cate's inner self that could not be reached to reason. The Avery question appeared to be making its way to the loss column.

On that following Saturday, Neely and Avery were together at the same restaurant by the river. It was a beautiful evening, the full moon chose to float in a shimmer over the river's moving water which seemed to separate itself into tiny ribbons uneven and lovely.

Avery reached across the table to touch Neely's hand. With all the courage he had, he said, "Neely I want to marry you."

In that instant, everything that had happened over the past dozen years seemed to revisit her consciousness. For a time she could not speak. After a considerable silence, Neely looked at Avery with love and respect but said, "Avery, I cannot marry you, and after tonight, I cannot see you again." She touched his hand. "I care too much to say yes. I have Cate and I will likely have her forever. I will not put you in a place where you are rebuffed, insulted, and even abused. Now, I must go."

Chapter Twenty-Three

More than ever, Neely recognized the unimaginable repercussions of autism. She realized that it does touch every aspect of the lives of those living within its control. Its severity determines the demands on the caregivers. For twelve years, Neely knew the difficulty of her situation and the severity of Cate's condition. Not until she had the opportunity for a life partner that included the normal things that loving someone offered did she fully understand the difficulties of her choices. The next few months were filled with questioning. It was difficult not to answer the phone or make a call herself.

She was dizzy from attempting to understand how to approach Cate. She fought to prevent her own anger. "Shouldn't I be allowed to have more?" she thought. This confusion became anger and the anger became anxiety, then panic. Her feelings and thoughts were circular; each time she reasoned the logical outcome. She fought against blaming Cate and she finally managed to forgive her for what she had done, realizing that it was Cate fighting for what she was unwilling to give up. To her, it was the loss of her mother. She was smart enough to see what that possibility meant to her.

Neely found herself spending more and more time in the parlor, sunk deep in blue velvet and depression. She had given up her panic but she could not shake the sadness. She read and reread poems by the Swedish poet and psychologist Tomas Tranströmer who was thought to have Asperger's. In his poem "Standing Up," he said, "It's been a hard winter, but summer is here and the fields want us to walk upright."

If only she could have made Cate understand.

Chapter Twenty-Four

Neely was in no way prepared for the day's mail. The stationery was familiar as was the return address. She had seen her mother write many notes on the monogrammed sheets, so properly embossed with her initials in white on white. She could recall having been sent out of the house in order that these notes be efficiently done. She even imagined that she could see her mother at her desk writing this letter, warning her to stay outside and play until she was finished.

She carefully placed the letter in her pocket. Asking Jenny to bring her some tea, she made her way into the parlor. She speculated as to what this letter might say. Were her parents her coming for a visit at last? Did they regret not seeing her or the children? Was her mother seeking forgiveness? Neely's hands shook as she opened the letter.

Dear Anna Lee,

I thought you would want to know that your father died. The funeral was held two weeks ago and he was buried in the Burke family plot here in Covington. He had been ill for some time. I hope this letter finds you well.

As ever,

Mother

Neely collapsed into the chair, not even aware enough to hope it was there to catch her. She trembled as she reread the brief note. The words, "as ever" seemed a vague, ambivalent assurance, as if it was affirming the behavior to which she had adhered for more than a decade. She simply could not believe what she read. How could it happen that she was not even included at the funeral of her own father? She thought back on her life with him, his harsh demanding persona, his insistence on control and having his way to the extent that he would turn his back on his own child for falling in love with a Catholic. How could he have died not knowing or seeing his own grandchildren? How do such tragedies occur?

She was white with rage yet racked with sadness. How could her mother deliver such a message in a short note on her fancy stationery? Grief was added to insult and injury, but oddly, her grief was not particularly about the death of her father; it was about the death of that family. In retrospect, it was almost as if there had never been a real family. She realized now how much she had resented her parents' total involvement with the church and the refusal to see any other religion as having value, as well as their willingness to turn their back on her. The loss of her parents and at least a semblance of love had happened so many years ago. Looking out the window, she saw Cate carelessly throwing a stick up into a tree, oblivious to any other thing that was happening. Cate was in her world and for the moment, happy.

"How fickle life can be," she thought. "You are born into the world innocent to the possibilities both good and bad and you are expected to endure. Perhaps that is the life lesson I was meant to learn," she reasoned. She had with certainty been given countless opportunities in which she could learn to carry on.

Neely thought back over her life before and after marriage, after the birth of her children, and she realized that she had endured, not easily at times, but she was still standing. The pain she experienced from reading her mother's note for a third time was slightly mitigated by the recognition of the strength she had been required to maintain. She thought to herself, "I suppose I can and will do this…this thing I have been asked to do, that I must do, to remain steady in the ongoing adversities that have become my life."

She thought of her son, Michael, and his accomplishments at the Millford School. She reminded herself of his interest in the violin and his dedication to mastering the instrument. She thought of Cate, her art work, her love for Jenny, Miss Ava, Pearl, and of the times when she was quiet and loving, when she obviously wanted to be loved in return.

Neely's sadness turned from the loss of her father, that family of her birth, and the brief formality of her mother's note, to the disconnect represented by the many years that she had not seen her parents, but most of all that they had never seen her children. What would they have thought of the twins? Of Michael? Of Cate? She wished for Sean Michael and then, and then... she wished for Avery.

Not many of Neely's wishes were granted but she said to herself, "I can do this." She held the note, closed her eyes, and again said, "I can do this."

Chapter Twenty-Five

J enny had the flu and was resting in bed in her cottage. Pearl was nursing her through and keeping up with all the chores for both. Neely dressed hurriedly so that she might help Pearl in the kitchen. Even though Neely had not done much cooking through the years—as Jenny wouldn't have allowed it— she did know how. Jenny had made sure she could cook, but she would not turn it over to Neely or to anyone else for that matter. That certainly included Grace who was showing signs of early dementia and was likely to forget to put the baking soda in the cake or worse, leave the pan on the fire. So Neely was prepared to help out when needed. This was a day when she was needed.

Flying hurriedly down the stairs, Neely missed the last step and as she went down she crashed her head against the last rung of the banister. She was unconscious only briefly but, when she opened her eyes, there stood Simus, speaking to her and saying, "Oh dear, oh dear, oh Ma'am you've gotta' wake up." She sat up and then leaning on his reliable shoulder, made her way to a chair in the kitchen. She felt she was just fine but the fall had caused both pain and reflection.

More than once over the past twelve years Neely had thought, "What if something happened to me? What would happen to my children?" She had been more fortunate than many dealing with an autistic child. She had the O'Malleys, Jenny, Pearl, and Simus. She knew how lucky she was to have them. They had been there through the roughest of times, but the years were getting by and time had taken its toll on all of them. Neely herself felt that she had aged beyond her years. Her lovely auburn hair had made its way to a premature silver and while it was lovely, she knew that it had come too soon and for all the wrong reasons.

Still the question haunted her. Not unlike other parents of autistic children, she began to research the possibilities. The fact to remember was that autistic children become autistic adults. She knew of autistic people who had a job; some were somewhat independent and lived in group homes. She knew that as long as Grace O'Malley and Virginia Bird Drummond had a breath of life left in their bodies, Cate would go nowhere. The O'Malleys were getting old and though they were strong, they would not be there forever. Pearl's spirit was willing but the emotions were not able. Simus would do anything needed but there were many times in a young girl's life when a woman was needed. That would be especially true as Cate entered her teen years. She was about to encounter new experiences that she would not understand and would likely cause great anxiety.

Michael was also entering that confusing time when hormones take charge. He was beginning to harbor more and more resentment that a large portion of his life was sacrificed in favor of Cate. He was heard to say, "I hate autism, I want no part of it." He was hesitant to bring his friends into the home. Cate was more rowdy than ever and exhibited some amount of jealousy when it came to those she lived with. Her outbursts were more intense, louder, and more likely to come from the many movie scripts she called upon when expressing herself and her displeasure. She had even learned a few dirty words. Yet Michael still defended her to anyone who might be critical of her and her behavior.

Neely knew they were facing the complexities of the teen years, the typical behavior of that time likely to be exacerbated by the combination of puberty and autism. Neely, realized this and could see the difficulty, which seemed more like a call to battle in the new stage they were about to enter.

Michael was popular and had many friends. Cate wanted to be around other people, but strictly on her terms. She was still in her world and the slightest jarring of that world could set off an unpleasant reaction. She was most content watching her movies, using their words to speak, and in general getting her way. Michael found comfort away from home. His continued friendship with his headmaster had become a very personal bond. Neely knew that she could stay at Kilhaven forever. As long as she and her children were there, they were cared for and safe. She just had to hope that everyone concerned would enjoy longevity, herself included.

still to her world and the shadows lurking of that world could so off an unpleasant reaction. She was most content watching her movies, using their words to speak, and in general getting her way. Michael found comfort away from home. His continued friendship with his headmaster had become a very personal bond, Nicely knew that she could stay at Kilhaven forever. As long as she and her children were there, they were cared for and safe. She just had to hope that everyone concerned would enjoy longevity, herself included.

Chapter Twenty-Six

Neely decided to get some things done. It had been weeks since she had seen Avery, and she felt the need for a sort of a mental and physical spring cleaning. She purged her closet, ridding herself of old clothes that someone else needed more than she. She repainted her chest of drawers and put in new lining. In the parlor, she rearranged the furniture and then put it right back where it had been. She polished all the silver in the dining room and wondered why the silver service was left out when no one ever used it anymore. Ladies' tea parties were no longer a part of life at Kilhaven and the silver was just something else that needed attention.

Then she turned her thoughts to the day's lessons with Cate. Cate's interests were limited to watching movies and painting pictures, but there was much learning that could be accomplished from both. It would have pleased Neely if there could have been some semblance of conversation about the art. Even now with praise, Cate would pull away.

Some of the artistic images were benign while others were drastic and bold and seemed to represent turmoil. She could hardly keep Cate in drawing tablets and the "art collection" exceeded all expectations. Embracing the notion that one must bloom where one is planted, Neely decided that what they were doing was working and they would stick with it. Cate skipped off to find Jenny and Neely took a moment to sit. By late afternoon she found herself alone. Everyone at Kilhaven had found it necessary to be somewhere else.

It had rained off and on all day. The clouds were unwilling to let anything through and it had a profound impact on Neely. It was one of those extremely rare days when she was absolutely alone and the clouds seemed to have made their way into the house and perched themselves squarely on her shoulders. She treasured such isolated moments when she could stop and read or think or just do nothing. However on this day it was not so.

She was restless mentally and physically. She moved to the back porch and opened a book which she quickly discarded. "Well, Anna Lee O'Malley, you might as well give in and just let your mind find its way to the place it is trying so hard to go," she said to herself. Looking out through the oaks and elms, she let herself fall into her thoughts. She tried not to think about certain things. She bounced around mentally, first pretending that Sean Michael was alive, that both her children were perfectly well, and that her hair was still auburn.

With those pleasant thoughts, she dropped off to sleep. In her dream she was a young woman back in her parents' home. Her father was kind and her mother was strong. They approved of her Catholic husband and they saw the children often. But still Sean Michael had died and Cate was autistic. In her dream state she reasoned that she could have some of what she wanted but not all of it. What difficult choices—what to keep and what to let go.

The dream became troublesome, even disturbing and as she fought her way out of what was becoming a nightmare, she thought she heard a loud noise. Emerging from her sleep she realized it was simply someone knocking at the front door. In a haze, she stopped to pick up her book, which had fallen to the floor, and made her way toward the door.

It seemed as if it took forever to get there, and she was puzzled as she was expecting no one. The knock came again, this time with a bit more authority. Neely opened the door and there was Avery. Standing straight and tall, he looked at her squarely and, without hesitation, he said, "I am here and here I will stay. We will do this together."

Neely touched his hand.

Chapter Twenty-Seven

Neely heard the back door slam. That old door with the squeak warmly announced when someone was coming or going. They had decided long ago that the squeak of that old rickety back door was welcome and dependable. It was Cate running ahead of Jenny.

Cate stopped in her tracks when she saw Avery and it was as if all the air in the room had been sucked out; hardly enough to breathe for the three who found themselves suddenly confronting each other. Turning from the direction from which she had come, Cate ran back out the squeaky kitchen door and out to the barn. Neely slipped free of Avery's hand to pursue Cate, dreading what she knew was to come.

When Neely found her she was hiding behind the hay bales in one of her favorite spots to draw and paint. She had already started to paint and she would not look at her mother. With a steely determination, she turned her back on Neely and continued to draw.

As they sat on the dusty floor of the barn, there was a deafening silence between them; they could hear only the cries of the new calves in the pasture, a sound that reflected their own emotions. Neely thought, "Where is that beautiful sound of the cowbells? Why only the cries?" For some time, she sat and watched Cate furiously and deliberately use all her colors with harsh broad strokes. Neely said nothing. Sitting on the floor in silence she hoped the right words would come to her.

The sun was beginning to set. The crickets and cicadas combined their sounds to present their evening chorus. The hum and staccato were most welcome as it was now the only sound to be heard. Shadows grew long in the barn. Neely tried to think of what to say. What would Cate hear? Time seemed to drag. For Neely it was agonizing. Finally, it came to her. The words were Cate's words and Neely reasoned they were her best chance to be heard. With tenderness and love Neely reached out and gently touched Cate's shoulder. She said ...

"May I call you Alice?"

In the distance, Neely heard the faint sound of the cow bells. Cate slowly turned toward her mother.

Appendix

The following artwork was created by the child who served as the model for Alice. Within its circles, lines, and colors there is reasoning, meaning, creativity, and communication.

RESOURCES
For more information on autism, the following sources are of great value.

AAPC Bookstore*
AAPC Publishing, Inc.
11209 Strang Line Rd., Lenexa, KS 66215
1-877-277-8254 | 913-897-1004
www.aapcpublishing.net/bookstore.aspx

This store carries most books that have been written on autism. A trove of information.

Autism Asperger's Digest
PO Box 2257, Burlington, NC 27216
www.autismdigest.com

Autism World Magazine
http://www.autismworldmagazine.com

Autism Spectrum News
18 Purchase Street
Framingham, MA 01701
508-877-0970
www.mhnews-autism.org

Autism Society
4340 East West Hwy. Suite 350
Bethesda, MD 20814
1-800-328-8476
www.autism-society.org

Autism

and the
Autistic Jumble

Cate

(Alice)

Jenny

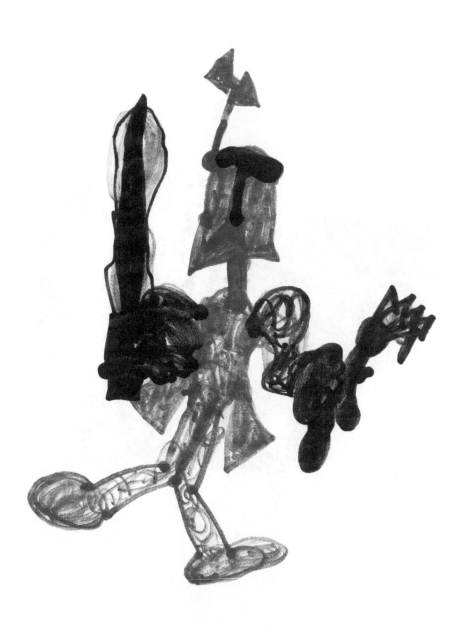

Neely

Sean Michael
O'Malley III

The O'Malleys'
Kilhaven

The Twins

The Oaks and
the Elms

Christmas at
Kilhaven

The Little Mermaid

The Tea Party

The Runaway Bunny
(and his mother)

Avery Milford

We are still here...

Autism
and the Autistic Jumble

Broken Heart Table (see page 32)

Broken Heart Table (see page 32)

About the Author

Beverly Tucker, PhD

Beverly Tucker did her graduate studies at Texas Woman's University. After completing her doctorate in Social Psychology and a year of post-doctoral continuation in psychotherapy, she was appointed Clinical Director of the Medical Education and Research Foundation in Fort Worth, Texas. Dr. Tucker later established her own private practice.

Having moved to Lexington seventeen years ago, she now combines her interests in human behavior, historic preservation, art, and writing.

It was in a professional setting that Dr. Tucker met the mother of the autistic child that was to become the inspiration for this book, *I'm Not Alice, I'm Alice.* This mother's courage, insight, and endurance is a model for all parents who are coping with an autistic child.

The story is a combination of enlightenment and example for all those who wish to understand and respond to the complexities of autism.

Dr. Tucker is the author of *Blackberry Winter* and *The House on Fuller Street.*

CPSIA information can be obtained at www.ICGtesting.com
Printed in the USA
LVOW01*1820131014

408491LV00001B/1/P